Refrigerator Cake

Short stories by Dickson Telfer
Illustrated by Amy Brownlee

Refrigerator Cake
Dickson Telfer
© 2014
All rights reserved — Dickson Telfer

Fledgling Press Ltd,
7 Lennox St.,
Edinburgh,
EH4 1QB

Illustrated by Amy Brownlee

www.fledglingpress.co.uk

ISBN: 9781905916870

Printed by Bell & Bain Ltd, Glasgow

Dickson Telfer lives in Falkirk with his girlfriend and two dogs. He works in Learning Development in Higher Education and spends most of his Saturdays following East Stirlingshire F.C. When not writing, working or watching silky football, his likes to attend, organise or perform at live literature events, walk his dogs in picturesque seaside villages and find excuses to avoid painting outdoor wood.

Amy Brownlee is from Edinburgh but currently lives in Dundee where she studies Illustration at Duncan of Jordanstone College of Art and Design. Other than drawing, she enjoys reading and watching films. She occasionally ventures into the outside world to fuel her coffee and art materials addiction.

Contents

Walkies

"Look, why don't you take the dog for a walk? We're just getting under each other's feet here. I'll carry on with the unpacking and try to make some room. You go and get some fresh air – take yourself and Pebbles away from all this chaos for a bit."

"Are you sure, honey?" I lift a box with QUENTIN printed on it, wishing I'd been more specific with my marking.

"Yeah. Poor dog must be bursting for a pee anyway," Joelle says, biro in mouth, opening a box of pots, pans and kitchen utensils which she quickly closes and scrawls 'kitch' onto.

"Okay. Do you know where her leash is? In fact, forget I asked that, it's in my white jacket pocket."

" . . . "

" . . . "

"Why are you still standing there?"

"Do you know where my white jacket is?"

"For heaven's sake, isn't it in the car or something? Or maybe in that big green box with the jackets and things? God, I don't know. What makes you think I know where everything is?"

"Okay, okay." I hold up my hands. "I'll find it, I'll find it. I was only asking."

"Sorry," Joelle says, momentarily closing her eyes. "It's just all this clutter. It's getting on my nerves. I feel like we've been at it for hours and we're getting nowhere."

"I know, I know. Okay, I'll leave you to it." I side-step my way out of the living room into the hall. "Pebbles? Pebbles? Come on, girl. Walkies!"

Pebbles runs out of the bedroom with a piece of cardboard in her mouth, tail wagging. I love how her excitement for dinner and walkies never wanes. Being a dog must be so much simpler than being a human.

"Hello, trouble, what have you been chewing?" Her tail drums off a cardboard box, her expression shifting subtly from excitable to mischievous.

"Drop it." I point to the floor. She lets go and, as the cardboard falls to the hideous swirly carpet, I notice it has a Q on it. I pick it up and walk into the bedroom, Pebbles' golden tail shedding hundreds of tiny hairs onto my navy trousers. In the bedroom, I easily find the box she had begun to dissect.

"Aw, good girl!" I say, patting her head.

"Don't tell her she's good for chewing the bloody boxes!" Joelle shouts from the living room.

"But it's the box with my white jacket in it," I shout back. "She must've sensed what we were talking about!"

I hear Joelle muttering something to herself, but I can't make it out over Pebbles' tail drumming off the vacuum cleaner. I take the jacket out of the box and check the pockets for the leash. Along with a small nylon bag of doggie treats and a couple of poo bags, it's there as I'd expected. I attach it to Pebbles' collar, put on my jacket and we weave our way to the front door.

"Bye, honey, back in 40 minutes or so."

"Bye, have fun," Joelle says, but she doesn't sound very genuine.

As I walk along the road, Pebbles looks up, eyes shining,

her gait proud, tail in the air, trotting along as happy as any living creature could possibly be.

"Where shall we go, girl? Let's see what's around here, shall we?"

After we've pounded the pavement for a few minutes, I see a field on the other side of the road and decide to cross and investigate. Once we're over, Pebbles sits patiently on the narrow grass verge, undeterred by cars speeding by only a few yards away.

"Well, girl, I don't see any sheep or cows. This should do us fine, eh?"

She looks up at me, her body poised, ready to leap up onto the little stone wall.

"Go on then," I say, and she leaps up and jumps off into the field. I swing myself over, pick up a stick and throw it as far as I can.

"Go get it, Pebbles!"

She bounds after it like it's the first time she's ever chased a stick; like her life depends on it; like bringing it back to me is the most important, rewarding and joyful thing she could ever experience.

Humans could do with sticks sometimes, I think to myself.

She runs back, wind in her face, grunting with delight. She drops the stick but before it lands on the grass, she begins to pee.

"Aw, Pebbles, you could've peed before you fetched the stick, pal."

She looks up at me with a slightly embarrassed face. I think how I'd feel if someone started talking to me while I was peeing, and walk away to let her finish in peace.

I walk across the field, throwing the stick, breathing the

fresh air, happy to be out of our new, smaller, house. I do an occasional three-sixty glance just in case a herd of cows or an angry farmer appears, but see nothing.

Once we get to the other side of the field, there's an identical small stone wall. On the other side is an empty road running through what looks like extensive parkland.

"Aw, Pebbles, look at this! This is perfect, isn't it?"

She wags her tail and leaps up onto the wall, stick in mouth.

"Just a minute. Staaaay."

I clamber over and double-check for traffic. But the place is deserted.

"Okay, come on then, girl." She jumps off the wall and darts towards the grass. I take out my phone and text Joelle.

> Found a great place for Pebbles.
> Think we're going to be great here
> hon x

We walk up a hill and past a two-storey derelict building made from sandstone. It looks like an old residential home. My phone beeps. I throw the stick for Pebbles and have a look. It's just spam from a bank I don't even use. I press delete and put it back in my pocket. When I look up, Pebbles is running towards me, but nervously looking behind her at the man in the blue jacket running after her.

"Hiya," he shouts from a few metres away, raising his hand in the air. Pebbles drops the stick at my feet and stands behind me, peering round my legs as he approaches. I raise my hand in return so not to appear unfriendly.

"Your dog's gorgeous," he slurs, a little out of breath. "Is it okay if I pet him?"

4

"Eh . . . yeah, sure. She's a girl dog, though."

"Oh, sorry." He kneels down. "What's his name?"

"Pebbles."

"Hiya, Pebbles, come here, pal."

"It's okay, darling," I say. "Go and say hello."

"Hello, boy. You're a cracker, aren't you?" He ruffles her hair and pats her hard – perhaps too hard, like it's crossing the boundary between patting and hitting.

"She's a girl dog, remember," I say with a smile. He looks up, chin glistening.

"Yeah, I know, you've told me that already."

" . . . "

" . . . "

"Lovely day," I say.

"Sure is." He massages Pebbles' neck, really digging his fingers in. And despite his vigor, she allows him to pet and admire her, trusting me entirely. After a few moments of silence, and two hefty pats on the back, he stands up. "I've got problems with my feet," he says.

"Oh, right."

"See what I was doing to your dog's neck there? That's what I need done to my feet. The nurse I've got just now doesn't do it right, but the nurse I had before her, Susie, she was brilliant at it. She used to put me on this bed in the other room and I'd hang my feet over the edge, right, and then she'd sit at the end of the bed and lather her hands with this special lotion, and then she'd massage my feet, like, really hard, and get right between my toes. Awwwwww, it was amazing." Arms wide and palms facing up, he looks to the sky, eyes half-closed, a fresh trail of saliva leaking from his mouth. "But the nurse I've got now doesn't do it properly. She's useless. It's like she barely touches them at all. It'd be like me petting Pebbles like this." He reaches over and strokes her once on the head. "I mean, what's the point of that, eh, boy?"

"Hmmm," I say.

"You've got to get the hands right in there, right between the toes. Like Susie. With the nurse I've got just now, right, one time I said to her 'have you started?' and she said 'yes, Eric, I have' – that's my name, Eric – and I said 'well you could've fooled me'." He laughs hard – short, sharp bursts – as white bubbles coat his chin. I nervously laugh along. He wipes his chin with the sleeve of his jacket.

"Well, Eric, Pebbles and I better get going, but it was nice to– "

"What way are you going?"

I point forward. "Eh, this way."

"Aw, great, me too, I'll walk with you for a bit."

"Eh . . ."

"Can I throw the stick for Pebbles?"

"Eh . . . yeah . . . yeah, okay."

He picks up the stick and tries to throw it, but it slips from his grasp on the backswing and cracks onto the road.

"Oops, try again," he laughs. "Are you ready, boy?"

He throws it successfully this time and it's actually quite an impressive throw. Pebbles races towards it, tail wagging, coat flowing in the breeze.

"So what's your name?" Eric asks as we begin walking.

"Eh . . . Chris. I'm Chris."

"It's nice to meet you, Chris, I'm Eric. I don't think I've seen you round here before. Are you new?"

"Yeah . . . yeah, I am."

Pebbles drops the stick at our feet.

"Aw, good boy," Eric says, picking it up. "Is Pebbles a golden labrador?"

"Golden retriever. They look similar but the difference is in the coat. Labs have shorter coats and Pebbles' coat is long. That's what makes her a retriever."

"I've got problems with my feet," Eric says.

"Yeah, you were saying."

"The nurse I've got just now doesn't do them properly. She just doesn't put enough into it. My last nurse, Susie, aw, she was brilliant, just brilliant. She used to do this." He throws the stick then raises his hands and mimes Susie's massage technique, edging into my space. "And awwww, honestly, it was amazing. Right between the toes. When she did it, I thought I was in heaven – like, actual heaven. But the nurse I've got just now, she just doesn't do it right. I don't think she likes me 'cos I tell her she needs to do it like Susie. Susie was brilliant. Right between the toes." He lifts his hands to just below my chin, continuing his mime.

"Yeah, well, maybe she'll get better." I quicken my pace. Pebbles drops the stick and I swiftly reach down, pick it up and throw it.

"No. No chance. No-one can beat Susie. She was brilliant. She just had a knack for it, you know?"

"What is it that's wrong with your feet anyway?" I ask.

"They're just not right. You know . . . just not right. They're not like everyone else's. Everyone else's are fine. But not mine. Mine are just not right."

"Are they sore just now?"

"No, they're fine. Why would they be sore?"

"Well, 'cos I thought you had problems with them?"

"Yeah, I do."

"But they're not sore?"

"No. Why would they be?"

" . . . "

" . . . "

Pebbles drops the stick so we have to stop.

"Good boy," Eric says, and he reaches down and picks it up. He puts his whole body behind the throw as if he's throwing a javelin at the Olympics, only there's no grunt. Pebbles looks at him as if he hasn't thrown it, and it's only when she hears it landing in the distance that she turns and gallops towards it.

"So they're never sore then?" I say.

"What?"

"Your feet."

"No."

"But I thought you had problems with them?"

"Yeah, I do. I've got problems with my feet."

"So what's the problem then?"

"My new nurse. She just hasn't got the knack. But my last nurse, Susie, awwww, she was brilliant. She used to get right between my toes."

From bushes on our right hand side, two men run towards us, about 50 yards apart, the first wearing a puffy red and black jacket, the other a blue tracksuit top.

"Doctor! Doctor! He says he's going to beat me up 'cos I don't support Rangers! Go and tell him not to beat me up 'cos I don't want to be beat up . . . but I don't want to support Rangers either," the first man shrieks, pointing over his shoulder at his assailant. He cowers behind me, gripping my right arm, shaking with fear.

"Doctor, he says that Rangers are crap!" the assailant shouts as he approaches. "And that's not true! How does he know if he's never been to Ibrox? He's always winding me up and I'm sick of it! I'm fucking sick of it!"

"Doctor, tell him to stop swearing at me! Swearing's not

allowed, Vince. You're going to get into trouble! Tell him, Doctor!"

"Whoa whoa whoa, just hold on a minute." I put my arm out. "You've got me all wrong here, I'm not a doctor."

"Are you not?" Eric asks, surprised. "So you don't know what happened to Susie then?"

"No, Eric, I don't know what happened to Susie."

"Ahhhh, you're just having us on, aren't you?" he laughs.

"Course he is," Vince says. "Look at his coat! And look at big-pussy-Roddy hiding behind him, just like he does with all the other doctors."

"Don't call me that!" Roddy howls, gripping my arm tighter.

"Look, honestly, guys, I'm *not* a doctor! I've just moved here. I'm just out walking my dog." I point over Vince's shoulder, pleased to see Pebbles ambling towards me with the stick in her mouth. She must've found some smells down where the stick landed.

"Ahhhhhhh! Dog!" Vince wails and he and Roddy quickly change places.

"Ha ha! Rangers are crap and the doctor's dog is going to bite you for threatening to beat me up," Roddy laughs.

Vince grips the loose fabric of the back of my jacket like it's the frame of a rollercoaster car. "Does your dog bite, Doctor? Does your dog bite? Does it bite, Doctor, does it bite?" he sputters, gripping onto me for dear life.

"Don't be silly," Eric laughs. "Pebbles is a lovely dog, isn't he, Chris?"

"Yes, she's harmless," I say as she approaches. She drops the stick and, looking confused, sits down and scratches behind her ear with her hind leg. Roddy dances in front of me, pointing down over my shoulder at Vince.

"Glory, Glory, Man United! Glory, Glory, Man United! Rangers are crap! Rangers are crap!"

"Oh my God, look at the claws on him," Vince whimpers. "And Rangers are not crap, Roddy. Man United are."

"It's a girl dog," Eric says.

"She's a bitch!" Roddy exclaims. "Vince's going to get clawed to pieces and then eaten by a vicious bitch! That'll teach you to threaten me, Vince! Glory, Glory, Man United!"

Vince grips me so tightly it feels like the zip of my jacket could tear like a sheet of soggy kitchen roll.

"You guys are nuts," Eric says, walking over to Pebbles.

"Glory, Glory, Man United. Vincey's going to die! Vincey's going to die!"

"Doctor, tell him to stop it! Tell him to stop it! Rangers!"

"ENOUGH!" I roar, stunning them into silence. Pebbles, tail between her legs, pads onto the grass and lies down. "I am Doctor Chris Stewart and I will not tolerate this nonsense!"

"I *knew* you were a doctor," Eric says, wiping his chin with his sleeve.

"Vince, I want you to let go of my coat. You have my word that Pebbles won't bite you. And Roddy, I want you to be quiet. No more teasing, okay?"

"Okay." Roddy looks at the ground like he's a schoolboy being told off for stealing someone's lunch money.

"Okay, Vince . . . Are you ready?"

"I think so," he says, letting go of my jacket. I slowly take a step to the left and turn so I'm standing between Vince and Roddy, like a boxing referee. Vince's hands are up by this throat, one clenched in a fist, his eyes fixed on Pebbles, whose chin is on the grass, looking away from us.

"Now, you guys need to say sorry to each other. Why

don't you try to be friends? You can still be friends with people who don't support the same team."

"I don't support anyone," Eric says, "and I'm both your friends. Eh . . . I'm your both friend."

"I'm sorry, Vince," Roddy says, looking up slightly.

"I'm sorry too, Roddy," Vince croaks, his eyes still firmly fixed on Pebbles.

"Okay, good," I say. "Now, can Pebbles and I continue our walk now that you two are friends?"

"Yes," Roddy says.

"Uh-huh," Vince says, and he turns and runs up the hill towards the derelict building, looking over his shoulder to make sure Pebbles isn't chasing him.

"Hey, Vince, wait for me. Let's go play draughts," Roddy shouts, bounding after him. But then he stops abruptly, turns round and shouts: "Hey, Doctor, who do you support?"

"Barcelona."

"Good choice! Not as good as Man United, though!" He kisses the crest on his jacket. "Wait for me, Vince!"

"Those guys are crazy, eh?" Eric says, shaking his head.

I take a tissue from my pocket and wipe the back of my neck. As I walk towards Pebbles, she stands up, shakes and stretches. When I return the tissue, I feel my phone vibrate.

> Sorry for snapping. Things looking better here now. Thats gr8 u found a good place 4 walkies. Jst started making lasagne. Jx

"Come on, Pebbles, time to get going, pal."

"I used to be a doctor, you know," Eric says.

"Is that right, Eric?"

Pebbles picks up her stick and walks by my side.

"Yeah, but I had to stop practicing once I started having problems."

"Oh, right."

"I've got problems with my feet, you see. If my last nurse, Susie, was still here, I could easy be a doctor again. Probably in a few weeks. You see, she used to lather her hands with this special lotion and massage my feet really hard, and get right between the toes, awwwww it was amazing."

I break into a jog. "What is it that's wrong with your feet, Eric?"

"They need massaged," he says, jogging alongside me. Pebbles looks up, tail wagging hard, thinking it's a game. "But the nurse I've got just now, she doesn't do them properly. Thanks to her, I don't think I'll ever be a doctor again."

"That's a shame." I increase my pace.

"Yeah, but if I could only find Susie," Eric pants, lagging behind, "then everything would be fine because she was amazing. She had this special lotion, right . . . Doctor, do you know where Susie is? Doctor, can you . . . slow . . . down?"

"Sorry, Eric, I've got to run, I've got other patients to see." I break into a sprint. Pebbles drops the stick and races alongside me, barking.

"Okay, well . . . if you see Susie . . . tell her . . . tell her from Eric . . . tell her from Eric to please come back."

I glance over my shoulder and see him hunched over, hands on knees, a string of saliva dangling from his mouth. I face forward and run, eyes damp, and think of Joelle, and home, and lasagne.

Naked Mole-Rat

I'm rarely happier than when I'm biting into the flesh of a champagne-soaked strawberry. I pick bottles of Lanson, Tattinger and Veuve Clicquot off the shelf and place them next to the two large punnets of fresh strawberries in my trolley. Mouth watering, I open one of the punnets, pick out a beauty and stuff it in my mouth. I don't check for members of staff. I mean, what are they going to do? I'm 92 for heaven's sake.

In the biscuit aisle, I look for Gold Bars, Fox's Classics and Double Chocolate Digestives. I remember reading how deceiving plain Digestives are when it comes to sugar and fat content, so the double chocolate variety must be doubly bad, if not more. I place two large packets in my trolley, but oops, one of the packets has a tear and a biscuit somehow manages to slip out and find its way between my thumb and forefinger.

Incredible the doctor said. *92 and in excellent health.* She looked like she couldn't believe it. I could barely believe it myself. Okay, I looked after myself when I was a young guy; actually, I looked after myself right up until Maggie died. But that was 24 years ago.

In the coffee aisle, I pick a ready-ground Colombian variety and a packet of beans from Ethiopia which I'll grind myself. I'll drink the Colombian with cream and brown sugar, but the Ethiopian black to appreciate its bitterness.

Ethiopian coffee is the bitterest I've ever tasted and I wonder if it's because they're bitter people. Disappointed at the lack of infrastructure in their country, frustrated at their inability to do anything about it. I bet none of them live to 92. I hate imbalance. Maggie bought me a jumper one Christmas which she'd had specially made. On the back was a set of scales and underneath in capital letters it said TYPICAL LIBRA. Still got it, actually. Wear it to bed sometimes.

I add a four pack of Cadbury's Boosts, two litres of Coca-Cola, two litres of Irn Bru, a few frozen pepperoni pizzas and a couple of microwaveable curries to my trolley and head for the checkout.

I place my bags at the end of the checkout.

"Would you like a hand to pack, sir?"

"No, I'll be fine, thanks," I reply.

"Eh, are you sure?" she says, looking at the bottles on the conveyor belt and then at my wrinkly, weathered face.

"I said I'll be fine."

"Okay."

She begins to scan my items, ignoring the fact a few have been opened. But after about a minute it's me waiting for her because she's had to look up the price for loose Chelsea buns. "Come on, keep them coming, hen. Would you like a hand to scan there, ma'am?"

We all laugh: me, the girl at the checkout and the people waiting.

"You're pretty impressive," she says, handing me my change.

"So are you – but take away the impressive," I say with a wink and a cheeky laugh. Her reaction tells me I've got away with it. Funny without being sleazy. Just.

I approach the cigarette counter as the only customer.

"Can I help you, sir?" asks a tall guy who reminds me of the actor Tim Robbins.

"Yes. Yes you can. I'd like some cigarettes please."

"Could you be more specific?" he laughs.

"C3," I say.

"Sorry?"

"You've played Battleships before, yes?"

"Eh . . . yes . . . a long time ago, though."

"Well, since the government has decided to make cigarettes more appealing to kids by hiding them behind little plastic flaps like Christmas presents, I can't see what's available, so if you pretend that the grid of flaps is a Battleships board, I'll have 40 of whatever's behind C3."

"Brilliant!" Tim Robbins laughs. He spins on his heels and traces his finger down and along the flaps. "This one?" he says, looking over his shoulder.

"Aye aye, Cap'n."

"Lucky Strike!" he announces and places two packs of 20 on the counter.

"I'd say I'm quite a shot, wouldn't you?"

We laugh. I hand him a £20 note and when he gives me my change, I stand tall and salute. Grinning, he returns a casual alternative, the kind used to acknowledge approaching friends. I sling the cigarettes into one of the bags in my trolley, glance at my watch and head to the car park.

As I wait for my taxi, I look at the cars dotted across the car park. It looks a bit like Battleships too. Lots of misses. A few hits. The group of six is a sink, I would think. But on a Battleships board there's no McDonald's litter; no brown paper bags just dropped out of doors or thrown out of windows; no paper cups and stripy straws strewn across the grid.

I look at some of the nicer cars. I've still got my licence, but there are far more cars on the road now than there were when I started driving. It's a different game out there these days. I'm better leaving the responsibility in others' hands, I think, plus I can't be bothered with all that tax, MOT, insurance and service carry on. At least if the taxi, bus or train breaks down, it's not me who has to fix it.

"Taxi for McEndrick?" bellows an overweight man wearing a white baseball cap, leaning over the handbrake to the partially open passenger window.

"Yes," I say, putting my hand up like a schoolchild, "that's me."

"I'll give you a hand, mate," he says, glancing at my trolley.

He pops the boot open and gets out of the car. I can't remember the last time someone called me mate and it fixes me to the spot with a smile. Maybe I still look hip and cool. Well, as hip and cool as a guy in his 90s can be. Mate.

The stench hits me as soon as I'm in the car. B.O.

"I can't stand this heat," he says, pulling out of the car park.

"That's what everyone says. And when it's cold, everyone complains that they can't stand the cold. People in this country are never happy. How old are you? 40-something? Surely it should be me who's complaining about the weather, eh? Not a young thing like you."

"I'm 38."

"Oh, right, sorry." I look out the window.

He takes the long way to get more money out of me. Probably thinks I'm senile or have Alzheimer's or something. We sit in silence, strangers in a confined space. He smells like rotten peaches. I imagine wasps flying in the sunroof and feasting on his armpits, stinging him as a lesson to wash properly – or at least keep a can of deodorant in the glove compartment.

"Is your wheel balance out a bit?" I ask, for no other reason than to take my attention away from the smell.

"No, mate, it's fine," he says in a monotone.

He drives alongside the inviting river and past my favourite greasy spoon cafe – Maggie's Diner. Not my Maggie, but I like it because it reminds me of her, and because she does the best bacon roll I've ever tasted.

"Can you go faster?" I ask.

"Got to stick to the speed limit, mate. Drivers can lose their badges for speeding, you know."

"Yeah, but this bit's pretty clear, wouldn't you say? And there aren't any speed cameras on this road. Come on! Overtake this slowcoach Corolla and give an old guy a bit of a thrill!"

"No way, mate, it's not worth it. Plus there's loads of corners on this road."

"Boring bastard!" I blurt, and he turns, surprise in his deep set eyes. "So, first of all, you complain about the weather, then you insult me by taking the long way to make an extra buck, and now you don't even have the decency to give an old guy a thrill. Well, thank you very much! Taxi driver of the year award for you!"

His expression is hilarious. But I remain dead pan. The Corolla turns left, leaving the road clear, but he doesn't speed up. In fact, he slows down.

"Are you sure the balance is right in this car? I think you should get it checked. I mean, you don't want to be putting paying passengers in danger, do you?"

"Says the guy who wants me to speed on a windy road,"

he sneers, shaking his head. Turning into Conway Court, he slows to a crawl.

"What number?"

"37," I say, "same as my age."

A patronising laugh escapes from his fat mouth.

"My mental age," I say, looking at him. But he doesn't look back.

"There you go," he says, popping the boot. I get out and unlock my front door. We transfer the bags from the boot to the hall, sweat dripping from our brows. I notice a bead of his sweat glisten on the cheap plastic of one of the bags and fear for the cauliflower inside.

"Okay, so that's £7.20," he says.

"Let's call it six quid," I say.

"Eh, no, I don't think so, mate," he says, eyes closed, laughing through his nose.

"Well, I *do* think so. Mate. You took the long route. The short route is six quid, so that's what you'll get. I usually tip a couple of quid too, but not to people who try to fleece me."

"Look, mate, the metre says £7.20, so the fare is £7.20. Now pay up!"

"And what are you going to do if I don't, eh? Hit me or something? Eh? Is that it? Well, that's fine, take your best shot, right here," I say, pointing to my temple. "Come on, what you waiting for, big guy? Give it your best shot. Fast and hard."

"I'm not hitting you, you crazy old fool! Look, just give me the fare and I'll be on my way."

I reach into my pocket and fish out six pounds. He takes it in his chubby hand and turns to leave.

"Wait a second," I say, reaching into one of the bags. "Here's your tip."

"Cheeky old bastard!" he says and, after examining it briefly, tosses the can of deodorant at my feet.

"Don't be so ungrateful! That's worth a couple of quid anyway!" I yell as he revs his engine. He gives me the fingers as he pulls away. I smile and wave.

Once I've put the shopping away, I bring in the washing, which, instead of smelling like lavender, like the bottle says, smells of barbecued meat.

I fill a bucket with ice and water and place the bottle of Lanson in it. I wash a couple of smaller strawberries, drop them into my flute and place it in the fridge. I open the Double Chocolate Digestives, sit at the kitchen table and munch one after the other. I work out from the loose packaging that I've eaten seven in a row. That's a lot of calories and a lot of grams of saturated fat, but I can't be bothered totalling up exactly how many.

Even after 24 years, I can still picture Maggie sitting across from me. She loved those pink wafer biscuits. Cup of tea, plate of biscuits, biro in her hand, crossword puzzle on the table; looking up occasionally, smiling, asking me about sea birds with six letters or fabrics ending in t.

I open the back door, sit on the doorstep and place a Lucky Strike between my lips. I glance down at the packet. SMOKING CAUSES CANCER it says. I strike a match and light it. Burning chemicals billow around me, blue and unnatural. I shake the match till the flame dies and then suck hard. The tip glows orange. When I pull it from my lips and inhale, I cough until my face turns purple.

I hadn't expected such an angry reaction, even though it's been several years. But with perseverance and a few less aggressive coughing fits, I get into a rhythm and am soon able to puff away. I smoke three in a row, spluttering

occasionally, my head light. When I stand up, I feel the Double Chocolate Digestives churn in my stomach. I lean over the sink and spit into the drain. After a few minutes of sipping water and spitting, I know I've won the battle. I am not going to throw up.

I pop the cork and pour a flute of champagne. The first sip is always the best, but this time the satisfaction is intensified as the bubbles eliminate the taste of tobacco, like little fizzy warriors using acid to destroy all things evil. The first glass disappears quickly so I pour another, taking care to avoid any overspill. There's nothing worse than wasted champagne.

I look at the two items of junk mail I left on the table before going shopping. The first is a leaflet for wireless broadband which I couldn't care less about. The only thing I could do with having wireless is the vacuum cleaner. I'm forever getting tangled up in the flex or wrapping it round furniture. The second is a promotional offer to subscribe to *The World's Strangest Animals* for half price. I turn the page to look at the sample and drop the pamphlet onto the table, alarmed at the hideous creature looking back at me. The phone rings.

"Hello?"

"Hiya, Archie."

"Oh, hi, Bobby."

"I just thought I'd give you a phone to see how you're doing."

"Yeah, I'm fine," I say, pouring another flute of champagne.

"That's good," he says, and I know what's coming next. "I'm not too great."

"Oh?"

"Yeah, my arthritis is playing up, plus I've got another ingrown toenail and the doctor's gone and changed my medication again, you know, for my thyroid problem. I don't see why, though, I mean surely it can't be a good idea to mess about with things so often."

"Maybe just looking for the best mix, Bobby," I say.

"Yeah, you might be right, Archie, but I'll tell you, I'm getting suspicious of that Dr Underwood, 'cos a few people I've been speaking to have said that he's not up to much. My pal, Harry, from the bridge club, well, he says Underwood's pretty useless."

"Oh, right."

"And you know what Harry's got?"

"No."

"A problem with his prostrate! So that's nothing to treat lightly, is it?"

"No," I say, through a half-mouthful of bubbles. "Listen, Bobby, I'm really sorry, but I'm desperate for the loo, can I call you back?"

"Oh, right . . . yeah, sure, Archie, that's fine. Speak to you later."

I hang up, finish my flute and sigh. Bobby's alright, heart in the right place, but all he talks about is ailments, doctors, hospitals, infections, medications, treatments, problems, appointments. It gets me down. He's 12 years younger than me too. All my real pals have been dead for years.

I hate this. I mean, why so much hair has to grow down there, I'll never know. And as the years go by, more and more hair appears where I don't want it, and disappears where I do. I'll probably be in here a while, untangling the gunge from the nest. I turn on the extractor fan and sit down. Here we go.

Fifteen minutes later, I pour a fourth flute, open the Fox's Classics and sit back down at the kitchen table. Maggie's still there, quite content, eating her pink wafers and filling in her crossword. I look again at the hideous creature in the pamphlet and read the blurb. It's a naked mole-rat, native to the drier plains of East Africa. They never emerge from underground and can live for up to 30 years. In a box with a red border and the heading MOST AMAZING FACTS are two bullet points. The first says 'Naked Mole-Rats show little signs of ageing and maintain near-perfect muscle structure into old age!' The second says 'Naked Mole-Rats don't get cancer!'

I look closely at the photograph and after a bit of examination, it's actually an interesting creature to look at. And quite funny. Like a penis with walrus-teeth. I could even stretch to cute, with its tiny beady eyes and button nose.

"Maybe I'm a naked mole-rat," I say to Maggie. "Or maybe that's what I was in a previous life, and I've kept its DNA."

I look through the replenished freezer for something for lunch, but nothing takes my fancy, plus I can't be bothered cooking now I've drunk nearly a full bottle of champagne. I pour the last of it into my flute, down it and decide to walk to Maggie's for a bacon roll. I fish out the strawberries and put them both in my mouth at the same time. Bliss!

I walk into Maggie's to discover someone sitting at my usual table, but I say nothing and sit at the table in the corner, by the window. A copy of *The Times* has been left, so I flick through it to see if there's anything of interest.

"Hello, Archie," Maggie says, order pad in hand, "we don't usually see you in here on a Wednesday."

"I know, but I couldn't stop thinking about your bacon rolls," I say, realising I'm slurring my words slightly.

"And look at that, someone's taken your table as well," she whispers, shielding her mouth with her pad.

"Ah, that's okay, darlin', I'm fine here. A change never hurt anyone, eh?"

"Well, as long as you're happy, Archie. We've got to take care of our long-term customers, haven't we? So, it'll be a bacon roll then?"

"Make it two. With plenty brown sauce!"

"Okay-dokey," she laughs. "And to drink? Just your usual white coffee?"

"Make it a latte," I say, raising a finger, "with three sugars."

"Right you are. Treating yourself today, are we?"

"Well, why the hell not?"

"Why the hell not indeed," she laughs.

I eat the first bacon roll quickly, my champagne belly growling, and take my time with the second, sipping my latte and flicking through the newspaper.

A shadow appears and I peer over the top of the newspaper to see a man in a charcoal suit standing before me.

"Yes?" I say.

"Are you Charlie?" he asks.

I glance over to the service counter but Maggie isn't there. I take a bite of my bacon roll and a dollop of brown sauce dribbles down my chin.

"Who's asking?" I say.

He sits down and puts his elbows on the table. I fold the newspaper and take a sip of my latte.

"You know who's asking, so don't play the smart arse with me," he says, running his hands through his short brown hair.

To give myself some thinking time, I take another bit of my roll and lean back in my chair, munching.

"Maggie's Diner, between 2 and 2.30pm, old guy at the window table reading a newspaper," he says, mirroring my casual posture.

"Who are you calling old?" I ask.

"You must be having a laugh." He shakes his head.

"Were you told he'd be eating a bacon roll with brown sauce and drinking a latte, and that the newspaper would be *The Times*?"

"I wasn't given that amount of detail," he says, screwing up his eyes.

My heart's beating hard. I glance out of the window, then over to the still unmanned service area. I take a sip of my latte and wipe the froth off my top lip. "Well, in that case it looks like your top boy is as much of a screw-up as you then, doesn't it?"

His face flushes with anger. "Look, have you got the gear or not, old timer?"

"Old timer? Old timer? What is this, some B-movie gangster flick you're living in, you pathetic waste of skin!" I lean forward and point in his face. "If you think I'm going to do business with people who can't even bloody-well communicate properly, you can think again. Away and take a run and jump!"

Secret Dens

David, Robin's here!

Coming!

Run in from garden. Dudley stays, happy with his chewstick.

Hi, Robin.

Hi, David.

Run up stairs to landing, open little door to secret den. Click on torch taped to rafter.

Wow!

Old carpet from Mum and Dad's room on floor, mattress with stripy pillows and duvet, all neat like hotel beds. Comics on one side – *Beano*, *Dandy*, *Victor*, *Cor!* – books on the other, biggest at the bottom, smallest at the top – *Huckleberry Finn*, *Noddy*, *Brothers Grimm*, *Famous Five*. Bottle of Fanta and plastic cups. Buckaroo, Connect 4, Guess Who? Gameboy with Super Mario, Tetris, Double Dragon. Spider-Man hanging from rafter on shoelace.

Cool posters!

Thanks. Dad got me them from the video shop.

This is sooooo cool. Do you sleep up here?

Sometimes. Slept here with Dudley on Friday, but he barked when it rained.

Ha ha, aw, poor Dudley.

Want some Fanta? Mum says it's short for Fantastic.

Ha ha, is that true?

Don't know. Want some?

Yeah, thanks. What was it like when it rained?

Funny.

Not scary?

No, just funny 'cos it was really loud.

Tsssssssssssss. Pour Fanta into plastic cups and let bubbles settle. Make sure not to spill any, else carpet will be sticky and Mum says it might attract beasties. Give Robin cup. Drink Fanta quickly and burp.

Ha ha ha ha

Ha ha ha ha

Want a game of Buckaroo?

Yeah, I'll set it up.

Set up Buckaroo and play best of three. Robin wins first game 'cos hand slipped. Win second though. Set up for deciding game.

David, are there spiders in here?

No. Why would there be spiders?

There's lots of spiders in our loft.

Yeah, but Mum hoovered after we put the carpet down. Are you scared of spiders, Robin?

No, of course not. Just don't think it'd be nice to have them near my bed.

Only spider near my bed is Spider-Man.

Look up at Spider-Man hanging above Robin's head. Think I see something move, but probably just eyes playing tricks. Robin wins third game fair and square. Jumps when I buck the donkey with the frying pan.

This place is really cool, though.

Thanks. Want to play Connect 4 now? Best of three?

*

Victor, David's here!

Run up stairs behind Victor to landing. Go to go into room.

David, up here. Come see my secret den.

Climb up ladder to attic room with proper lights, fitted carpet, bed with *Transformers* duvet.

Wow!

Pretty neat, huh?

Colour TV, Nintendo, Sega, video recorder. Ghetto-blaster, Discman, pile of CDs and tapes. Big box of action figures – *Transformers*, *Batman*, *Hulk*, *Masters of the Universe*, *Thundercats*. Bookcase of annuals, storybooks, videotapes. Model aeroplanes on chest of drawers. Mouse Trap, Hungry Hippos, Junior Monopoly, Frustration, Pop-up Pirate, Ker-Plunk! Glow-in-the-dark stars stuck to ceiling with double-sided tape, or sticky back plastic if on *Blue Peter*.

You okay, David?

Yeah.

So what do you want to do? Want to play Nintendo?

You got Super Mario?

Course I do.

Take turns to play Super Mario, but Victor much better than me so doesn't die as quick. Read *Topper* annual while he plays. Laugh at Beryl the Peril.

You not want to watch me play Super Mario, David? Look how far I am.

I am watching. Just looking at this too. Beryl the Peril's funny.

Think I'm going to get past this level without losing any lifes.

Can I have a drink, Victor? Got any Fanta? Or Vimto?

Maybe downstairs, but I'm playing this just now.

Okay.

Find *Fraggle Rock* cuddly toy between bookcase and wall.

This one's called Wembley, isn't it?

Hey! You're not meant to see that. Put it back!

Why?

Don't tell anyone, David. Aw, damn it! I've just lost my powers! See what you made me do!

Don't tell anyone about what?

About Wembley. Put him back.

Why? What's wrong with Wembley? I love *Fraggle Rock*.

Oh.

What's the orange one called again? With the purple hair.

Gobo.

Yeah, I like him the best. Want to play me at Hungry Hippos, Victor?

No, I want to play Super Mario. Look where I am. I've only been this far once, and I've still got loads of lifes left.

Watch Victor play Super Mario for a while, but get bored so say have to go to shops for Mum.

Oh, okay. But check how far I got!

Well done, Victor. Can I borrow this *Topper* annual?

Eh . . . my dad doesn't like me lending people things in case they don't bring them back.

*

Jay, David's here!

Walk along hall into Jay's room

Ha ha, Jay, you've got sticky tape on your face.

Oh, yeah, forgot that was there, ha ha. I'm making a castle.

Cool. What out of?

Cardboard.

Bed next to wall with faded orange duvet. Desk with lamp, jotters and comics, one *Dandy*, one *Topper*. Little pile of books – *Charlie and the Chocolate Factory*, *BFG*, *Little Vampire*. Crumpled poster of Duran Duran on wall next to wardrobe. Sticky tape, scissors and cardboard boxes on floor. Egg boxes, cereal boxes, boxes from local shop – Golden Wonder, Cadbury's Crunchie, Pampers, UHT milk.

Want some juice, boys?

Yes please, Mrs Carlton.

What would you like? There's apple and blackcurrant, Tizer or Fanta.

Fanta for me please, Mrs Carlton.

And what about you, Jay?

Apple and blackcurrant please, Mum.

Okay, I'll bring them through. You boys be careful with those scissors now.

Help Jay with castle. Manage to make moving door using string and cardboard flaps. Jay good at cutting windows and making them all same size. Use upside-down egg boxes for turrets.

Who's going to live in the castle?

I've got some Lego men in here.

Jay opens wardrobe, brings out small box of Lego, picks out three Lego men, all bald.

This one's you, David. And this one's me. Who will the third one be?

How about Robin?

Yeah, Robin. And this is our castle.

And we'll each have our own big cool rooms.

Yeah, and secret dens.

And we'll make plans to rule the world!

Drink huge glass of Fanta and burp. Mrs Carlton asks if I want to stay for dinner so can help Jay paint castle afterwards. Phone Mum. Says fine but home by 8 and remember to thank Mrs Carlton for her kindness.

A Breakfast Mess

I turn on my Blu-Ray player, go to YouTube and pick an R.E.M. concert from the mid noughties. Sipping a can of Irn Bru, I watch Michael Stipe cut some shapes, all tall and gangly, crazy purple stripe over his eyes like a superhero. *The Sidewinder Sleeps Tonite*, *Daysleeper*, *The One I Love*, *What's the Frequency, Kenneth?* Kello comes in at the end of *Orange Crush*.

"Alright, man?" he says.

"Yeah, man."

"Can I have one of those cans of Irn Bru?" He points at the freshly opened six-pack on the coffee table.

"Fire in."

He cracks one open and slouches on the sofa. "S'this?"

"It's an R.E.M. concert . . . obviously."

"Was only asking. You got a hangover or something?"

"Might have."

In the opening verse of *Man on the Moon*, Michael Stipe is kinda miming patting the heads of the crowd on the yeah, yeah, yeahs at the end of each line.

When the chorus kicks in the crowd goes bonkers, but it's a controlled chaos – one giant leaping monster. The camera zooms in on clusters of fans singing along, most getting the words right, but when the band merges into the second verse the singalong is patchier, although the crowd does seem to be enjoying Stipe's head-patting, most of them returning the gesture. I can't decide if that's cool or bizarre. Or both.

"Bit of a weirdo him, eh?" Kello says.

Second chorus and the crowd go crazy again, singing along at the tops of their voices as if they're trying to be louder than the band. *If you believe there's nothing up his sleeve, then nothing is cool.*

I laugh and look at the floor, shaking my head.

"This is too sweet for this time of day," Kello says, putting his can of Irn Bru on the coffee table. "You had breakfast?"

"Not yet. I don't think there's much in though."

"I'm sure there's cheese. I could make a couple of cheese toasties."

"Sounds good," I say.

When he returns, he places my toastie on the coffee table on a piece of kitchen roll and sits down with his in his hands. I watch bits of cheesy lava seep out between the slices, blotting the kitchen roll.

"Has he not already sung this one?" Kello asks.

"I rewound it. I love this song."

"Is this the song for that Jim Carrey movie? The one about the Elvis impersonator?"

I take a big bite of my toastie and a string of cheese sticks to my chin, which gives me a couple of seconds to think. "Eh, yeah, I think you're right. *Man on the Moon.* It had Danny DeVito in it as well, didn't it?"

"That's right," Kello says. "Hey, how come it was called *Man on the Moon* when it didn't actually have anything to do with the moon?"

"No idea, man," I say through a mouthful of stodge. "But I suppose *Trainspotting* doesn't have anything to do with trainspotting, does it?"

"True."

"How much cheese did you put in this by the way?" I pull another clump off my chin, but some sticks to my stubble.

"I just finished it off. Didn't think there was much point in putting a pokey little bit of cheese back in the fridge."

As Stipe sings about never-believers and ghosts for the offering, I take another bite of my toastie, but the bottom slice disintegrates and a huge cheesy blob falls between my legs onto the carpet.

"Shit!" I pick it up but it's like ectoplasm and oozes through my fingers onto the coffee table; my legs; the sofa. "Fuck's sake! What the hell is this? It's got a life of its own!"

Kello laughs as I wrestle with the cheese. He seems to have managed to finish his toastie with nothing more than some crumbs on his jeans.

The crowd cheers as the closing note rings out. I pick up the remote and press rewind, leaving a shiny residue on the button.

"Again?"

"Yes, again. I was too busy fighting with that toastie. What a bloody mess!" I fold the piece of kitchen roll twice and place the ball of cheese on it.

I manage to press play right at the point Mike Mills begins the opening riff. I watch the performance intently, fascinated by Stipe, drawn in by his conviction in every word. Kello's looking at his mobile phone.

"What's your take on the moon landings, man?" I ask him.

"Eh?"

"The moon landings. What do you reckon?"

"What do you mean, what do I reckon?"

"Well, do you think they happened?"

"What are you on about, man? Are you telling me you think there wasn't a man on the moon? Have you lost it or something?"

"No, I haven't lost it. Just think about it for a second . . . I mean, what about the lack of stars in the photos? Well, when I say lack of, I mean none, even though there aren't any clouds on the moon, which means stars should be perpetually visible."

Kello says nothing.

"Apparently the counter argument is that the light reflecting off the surface of the moon would have been too bright for the camera to capture anything in the background – but seriously, not even a twinkle?"

"I thought this song was about an Elvis impersonator? I'm sure I heard the singer mention something about Elvis in that chorus," Kello says, pointing at the TV.

"It's about Andy Kaufman, man. He *was* an Elvis impersonator."

"But I thought it was about that Jim Carrey film?"

"The film's *about* Andy Kaufman."

"I thought Andy Kaufman was a wrestler."

"He is. Was. He did lots of things."

"Did he go to the moon?"

"No."

"Then why's the film called *Man on the Moon*? Is it because people thought he was a space cadet?"

"No. Well, I don't think so, but who knows, maybe. Why don't you tweet Danny DeVito and ask?"

My head hurts. I finish my can of Irn Bru and crack open another. Kello's fiddling with his phone, hopefully not actually tweeting Danny DeVito. If it wasn't for my hangover, I could be enjoying this.

"Kello?"

"Just a second," he says, thumbs working away, slowly lifting the screen closer to his face, probably without realising. "Is there a problem with the internet? I can't seem to get online."

"There can't be. I'm watching this online through the Blu-Ray player."

"Yeah, but that's wired in through an ethernet cable. I think there must be something wrong with the wi-fi." He puts his phone on the coffee table and turns to face me. "Okay, shoot."

"*Man on the Moon* came out in 1992."

"Really? I thought Danny DeVito looked quite old in it."

"Not the film, the song," I say, pointing to the screen, even though R.E.M. are now playing *World Leader Pretend*.

"Okay, and?"

"The song is about Andy Kaufman."

"The wrestler?"

"Yes . . . the wrestler . . . and then when the Jim Carrey film came out in 1999, they called it *Man on the Moon*."

Kello scratches his head. "Okay, so let me just get this right. There's a song *and* a film about Andy Kaufman called *Man on the Moon*, and Andy Kaufman, who's a wrestler and an Elvis impersonator, and a man, has never been to the moon?"

"Correct," I say, wishing I'd never started this.

"Did he have anything to do with the moon landings? Like, was he part of the team who helped Neil Armstrong and, what's his name, Buzz . . . Lightyear?"

"Aldrin. No, he wasn't. There were no moon landings, man, it was a hoax," I say, exasperated.

"Is that what Andy Kaufman said?"

"I don't know! I don't even know if Andy Kaufman believed in the moon landings. Probably not. He was an intelligent, inquisitive sort."

"So why the association then? This is totally confusing."

"Let's just forget it, man," I say. I look down at the stain the blob of cheese has made on the carpet and make a mental note to get carpet cleaner when I go to the shops. Kello goes back to his phone. I take a big gulp of Irn Bru and burp. After a while, Kello gets up and leaves. I rewind the concert and watch *Man on the Moon* for a fourth time. I'd love to be Michael Stipe up there, making thousands of people jump around to a song many of them probably know nothing about. I reckon the majority of them believe in the moon landings too, or at least they haven't challenged it because NASA and the American government said it was so.

"One small step for man, one giant lie for mankind," I say to myself, and chuckle. Watching the third verse, I picture Andy Kaufman wrestling bears in heaven, looking down between rounds to say 'thank you very much' for writing a song with such a killer hook, and rejoicing in the fact that people will be singing about America's most elaborate lie for many years to come.

And then I wonder if I'm still a bit drunk from last night. I look at the ball of cheese and wonder how much fat is in it. Maybe R.E.M. were just taking the piss. I drink more Irn Bru and feel my belly rumble.

"Did you say *Trainspotting* doesn't have anything to do with trainspotting?" Kello says, walking back in.

"Yeah. Why?"

"Well, you're wrong. It's because trainspotting is just as addictive as heroin." He looks at his phone.

"Piss off. Where did you read that? Wikipedia?"

"No, it wasn't Wikipedia actually! Why do you always assume I'm a fucking idiot?"

"Do you really have to ask? You asked me if Andy

Kaufman had been to the moon! You probably don't even know he died in nineteen eighty . . . something."

I can tell by Kello's big, dozy eyes that his mind's working overtime for a comeback, the cogs spinning and whirring, some of them overheating with exertion.

"He might not be dead," he says, shrugging, looking out the window.

"Yeah, just like Elvis! Just like Richie from the Manics, Jimmy Hoffa and Michael fucking Jackson!" I throw my arms out in exasperation, knocking over my can of Irn Bru, which spills onto the coffee table and drips onto the carpet. "Fuck's sake! Look what you've made me do!"

I mop up what I can with my t-shirt then jog to the kitchen for a cloth. When I get back, Kello's still standing in the same spot, daydreaming. I drop to my knees, wipe the coffee table then start scrubbing the carpet.

"You're just rubbing it in, you tool," he says.

I stop dead and look up. "You what?"

"You're just rubbing the Irn Bru into the carpet. Don't you know nothing?"

"Anything."

"Whatever. And by the way, it was 1984. Andy Kaufman died on May 16th, 1984."

The Panini Thief

I join the back of the queue, about halfway up the stone staircase that leads up to the audition room, and look at my watch. Paper rustles as people look through their scripts. The smell of lived-in leather from the rotting Motorhead jacket in front of me catches the back of my throat as I admire the building's elegant Georgian interior.

"Excuse me, just to check. This is the open auditions for *The Panini Thief*, isn't it?"

Motorhead's ginger-bearded face is friendlier than his jacket led me to believe. "It is yes. Hide your lunch! Especially if it's a panini!"

I share his laughter, but his Adidas-clad pal is frowning, irritated by my interruption. I hold up a hand in apology and turn my attention to the intricate cornicing.

"So as I was saying," Adidas says, "I reckon I'm more of an ambivert than anything else."

"An ambivert? So, neither an extrovert nor an introvert, just somewhere in-between?"

"Yeah."

"Well, that's a bit of a cop-out, middle of the road, sit-on-the-fence type place to be, is it not?" Motorhead says in a kind of Barney Rubble voice.

I chuckle.

"Are you eavesdropping?" Adidas snaps, his frown deeper.

"Easy, easy," Motorhead intervenes, patting his friend on the shoulder. "We've had a tense couple of weeks," he tells me. "Auditions nearly every day, but no joy, not even extras stuff. It's been a long month, so we're just a bit hacked off."

"That's understandable," I say, avoiding eye contact with Adidas, who's now thumbing at his phone. "But please believe me, I wasn't eavesdropping, I was thinking of a joke I'd read in the paper earlier."

"Tell us it then," Adidas snorts, glancing down at his script.

"Calm down, man," Motorhead interjects. "Even if he was eavesdropping, it's not like we were talking about anything top secret, were we?"

"No, but it was personal. It's maybe why I'm not getting any parts."

"Right, so a white horse walks into a pub," I begin, managing to pluck a joke from somewhere. Adidas and Motorhead look at me. "The barman looks at it and says 'Hey, we've got a whisky named after you.' And the horse says 'What, Gerald?'"

Adidas manages a snicker while Motorhead blurts out a HA! of Brian Blessed proportions.

"Yeah, very good, mate, very good." Adidas shakes his head, but he's still smiling. "Where did you read that? *The Sun*?"

"Do I look like the kind of person that would read such a rag?" I laugh. "It was *The Daily Star*."

"HA!" Motorhead blurts again, although it's not quite the full Blessed this time.

"You know who you remind me of?" Adidas says, pointing in my face.

"Hugh Fearnley-Whittingstall?"

"Yeah! Hugh Fearnley-Whittingstall. Don't you think?" he says to Motorhead, pointing in my face again.

"Well, yeah, now that you mention it," he nods.

"Only without the glasses and a bit thinner, right?" I say.

"Well, without the glasses certainly."

Motorhead laughs but it's awkward, like bad acting. Adidas does that shrug rubbish comedians use to let the audience know they can laugh. Feet shuffle on stone as everyone moves up a couple of steps.

"So, which part is it you're auditioning for?" Motorhead asks.

"Jonathan Thacker," I say.

"Yeah, me too."

"Me too," says Adidas.

We look at each other, pistols for eyes.

A rocker wearing leather and denim with a ginger beard and ponytail – a cross between Bill Bailey and Lemmy.

A Britpop throwback with Damon Albarn hair, light blue jeans, black Adidas Sambas and matching tracksuit top.

And a glasses-free (and thinner) Hugh Fearnley-Whittingstall.

"Shouldn't be long now." I nod towards the audition room.

"Yup," Motorhead says, looking at his boots. Adidas scans the people behind me, squinting his eyes.

"Listen, I'm sorry, you guys were having a conversation about something earlier." I pull out my phone, mp3 player and earphones from my pocket. "Please, don't mind me." I turn my shoulder, push the earphones into my ears, mimic pressing a button on my player and fiddle with my phone.

"Right, so you think you're an ambivert?" "Yeah."

"And your agent thinks you're an extrovert?"

"Well, she didn't use that exact word, but yeah, I think so. You see, I get the extrovert bit from my dad because he's a singer, always chasing new opportunities, and the introvert bit from my mum because she's the calm, reflective type who's content with what she's got. Hence, ambivert."

"Okay, but you're still your own person, remember. No-one's an exact 50/50 mix of their parents. Plus don't you think saying you're an ambivert just sounds a bit–"

"A bit what?"

"Eh, fucking pretentious?"

They both laugh.

I flick through photos from last year's shoot in Greece, occasionally tapping my foot to no music.

"Here, what do you reckon of him going for Thacker?" Motorhead asks, flicking through his script.

"Who, Hugh Fearnley? I don't think he's got a chance."

I select one of the meditation CDs on my mp3 player and think of the shoots I did in Greece where I felt totally in control and everything ran to schedule. Making like the universal hand sign for money, I gently rub my thumbs up and down the recesses between my index and middle fingers, a technique I read about in a self-improvement book, and keep it going until I see Adidas strutting out of the audition room towards me.

"All the best," I say as he passes.

"Yeah, same to you, Hugh," he smirks.

"Next!"

Just before I walk in, I rub my thumbs and fingers together with such intensity that it leaves them tingling, almost burning.

From behind a desk, a bespectacled, balding man of about 50 looks at me with a smile, then glances down at a sheet of paper.

"Hi there, what's your name?"

"Hunter Carr."

He looks at the man on his left then the woman on his right. "Delighted to meet you, Hunter, we've heard great things from your agent."

"Well, I'll do my best to live up to it."

He smiles again and whispers something to the man sitting next to him. "And which part is it you're auditioning for today?"

"Jonathan Thacker," I say without hesitation.

"Excellent . . . Okay, Sam here will read the part of Donald Fox. Eh, I see you don't have a script with you. Sam, have we got a spare script we can–"

"It's okay, I don't need one."

"Oh . . . well, that's great. Okay, let's bash on then. In your own time, Hunter."

When I'm halfway down the stairs, I hear the clink of cutlery against glass. I turn to see the bespectacled man – Dennis Barker – at the top of the stairs, glass and spoon in hand, the final clink ringing out like a sustained piano note.

"Your attention, gentlemen, please."

The hubbub simmers to a silence.

"The part of Jonathan Thacker has now been cast. Those waiting in line, please be aware that you can only audition for the part of Donald Fox. Thank you."

Feet shuffle and eyes turn towards me. Disgruntled chatter swells as I walk towards the exit, where Motorhead and Adidas are standing, drinking cans of Sprite.

"You? – Hugh Fearnley Fucking Whittingstall – got the part?" Adidas growls. "Fuck's sake, I can barely afford to feed my dog."

I look into his angry eyes. "Well, you shouldn't have a dog then, should you?"

When I get outside, I send Celia and Michael a text with the good news and decide to celebrate with a brandy. The first goes down so well, I order another. A couple of guys drinking pints look over, one scowling. I feel my phone buzz in my pocket.

> Superb Dadio. Can't wait to tell all my pals ur going to be on the telly. Knew youd do it thou, ur from top notch stock. Hope u told the other wannabes to get it up them lol ☺ Proud. M

> You are amazing darling! So happy for you. Bottle of bubbly in the fridge def getting opened tonight! C x x x

As I get ready to leave, my phone rings. I look at the little phone symbol flashing next to the words Private Number. I hesitate, knowing it could be a call centre in India trying to sell me a new broadband package or insurance for something that doesn't really need insured.

"Hello?"

"Hello, is that Hunter?"

"Eh . . . yes."

"It's Dennis here, from the audition."

I swallow and stand up straight, as if I'm a teenager trying to convince a parent he hasn't been drinking. "Hello, Dennis."

"Listen, I just wanted to say that you absolutely fucking nailed it in there today. Blew me away. Sam and Helen too. We're really looking forward to working with you."

"Well, that's very kind of you, Dennis. Thanks very much, I'm really looking forward to wor–"

"It's not kind if it's the truth, Hunter. The truth is just the truth. Me saying that you fucking nailed it is the same as me saying the grass is green. It's FACT, and no matter how hard folk try, they can't change facts, can they?"

"Well, no," I laugh.

"Like NASA putting a man on the moon. That's a fact no-one can change – not a fucking soul – just like you being brilliant, Hunter. Honestly, my man, after we saw you we all agreed there was no point wasting everyone else's time. That's the first time I've ever done that by the way. It's not made me popular, but fuck it, time's precious, isn't it?"

"It sure is."

"Speaking of which, I better get myself out of here, got to pick my daughter up from the gym and get us home for our dinner. But before I go, I was wondering – are you available tomorrow night? It'd be good to touch base, read through some of the scenes, talk about the direction we want to take Thacker."

"Yeah, sure."

"Excellent. We'll do it at the Pink Flamingo Caravan Park. Gets us away from distractions. Families, mobile phones and all that stuff. Allows us to focus on the script and characters and nothing else, you know?"

"Sure. Yeah, that's fine. That's the caravan park about 20-odd miles up the coast, isn't it?"

"Yip, that's the one, yeah. Caravan 17 at the far end, 8 o'clock."

"Okay, I'll see you there tomorrow then. Looking forward to it."

When I hang up, I see I've got another text from Michael.

Meatball paninis for dinner! ☺

I listen to Fleetwood Mac as I drive up the coast. The really old stuff though – *Need Your Love So Bad*, *Albatross*, *Shake Your Money Maker*, years before Stevie Nicks joined the band. *Welcome to Pink Flamingo Caravan Park* the big sign says, decorated with huge flamingos smiling to the point of creepiness. I drive slowly to the back end, but have to brake hard when a black labrador darts out from behind a caravan in pursuit of a frisbee. I follow the numbers as I crawl – 23, 21, 19, 15? But between 19 and 15, isolated in the middle of a stretch of grass about 30 metres away, is what I assume is caravan 17. As I drive towards it, I see a BMW with the registration DEN 15.

"Hunter!" Dennis exclaims, throwing open the door of the caravan.

"Good to see you again, Dennis." I say, walking across to the caravan, hand extended. With a big smile, he gives it a good, firm shake and welcomes me in.

"Please, make yourself at home." He gestures towards the table at the far side of the caravan. "Can I get you a drink?"

"Eh, yeah, that'd be nice," I say, sitting opposite him.

"Okay, what would you like? I've got beer, cider, whisky, gin, vermouth, bourbon, and I think there's enough Shiraz left for one glass." He lifts the bottle up to the window. "Yip, definitely enough for a glass in there."

"What are you having yourself?"

"Oh, I think I'll have a cheeky little single malt on the rocks. I got given this bottle of Highland Park," – he picks it off the counter and looks at it admiringly – "and, you know, I'd forgotten how much I liked it. It's funny how that happens, eh? Things you really like just fade out of your life and you only realise how much you miss them when they pop up again."

"I like a single malt myself, so I'll join you in a Highland Park if that's okay."

"Of course it's okay! You're Jonathan Thacker, star of the show, aren't you? Would you like ice?"

"Eh, yeah, thanks."

"You know, you get people who say you shouldn't have ice in malt whisky," Dennis says, tipping large measures into dumpy glasses, "and if you're a *proper* whisky drinker, you should drink it from a *proper* whisky glass with nothing more than a dash of water to release the flavours. But you know what I think about them?" He places the glasses on the table and sits down.

"No," I say.

"Fuck them. Life's too short, don't you think? Far too short to worry about what people think about the way you drink whisky." He raises his glass. "To Scunthorpe!"

"Ah, a *Cracker* fan. To Scunthorpe!"

We down them and I feel the burn.

"You can't beat a bit of *Cracker*. Best crime drama in the history of television if you ask me," Dennis says, looking out the window at the empty stretch of grass. "Fabulous, fabulous stuff. What a character Fitz is, eh?"

"Absolutely. But I think Thacker is up there with him."

"Oh, come on, you're just saying that." He throws out a dismissive hand and takes off his glasses.

"No, seriously, he's an extremely well-written character."

"Yeah, maybe so." He plucks a little beige cloth from under a sheet of paper and cleans his glasses – "but Thacker is thin, mysterious and crafty, whereas Fitz is fat, obsessive and explicit."

"But they're both driven by the same thing," I say. "Addiction. With Fitz, it's gambling and with Thacker, well, it's obviously cocaine."

"You're right, Hunter. I hadn't thought of it like that before. Ching to Thacker is like spinach to Popeye. He wouldn't be the man he is without his fix, just like Fitz and his perpetual itch that to feel truly alive, to feel the blood racing through his veins, the place to be is that purgatory between winning and losing enormous, life-changing sums of money, the outcome placed on the shoulders of a living creature he doesn't know, doesn't care about and has no desire to meet."

"Exactly," I say.

"Of course I've thought about it before," Dennis says, putting his glasses back on. He looks through me, face stern. "It's pretty much where we got the idea for Thacker from. Difference is, gambling's legal. Cocaine isn't. It makes it more interesting, don't you think?"

I shift in my seat. "Well, yeah, I was just–"

Dennis laughs out loud, a spot of spittle temporarily darkening the margin of one of the sheets of paper on the table. "Hey, at least we're on the same page, Hunter! Another whisky?"

"Sure, why not."

"I assume you're staying over then, yeah?" Dennis clinks ice into the glasses.

"Am I? I didn't realise that was what you expected of–"

"Hunter, Hunter, Hunter." He sits down and places the glass in front of me. "I know you live in the country, but this is your second *large* whisky. Are you telling me you were going to drive home? Down that busy road? And risk your life? The lives of others?" He holds out his hands. "The life of *our* Jonathan Thacker? I don't do law breaking, Hunter. I like stories about it, sure, but fiction is fiction and the real world is the real world. Plus, if we're going to be bringing this character to life, it's important we get to know each other better, wouldn't you say?" He removes his glasses again and points one of the legs at me, like it's a second question mark.

"Well, yeah, sure, and it's fine, I always keep a spare change of clothes in the car just in case, so I'd be happy to stay, thanks."

"Excellent!" He replaces his glasses and gives me a big, closed-mouth smile.

"To Scunthorpe!" I raise my glass.

"Fuck Scunthorpe! Scunthorpe's a shithole!" Dennis barks. "And *The Panini Thief* is going to be far better than *Cracker*, far better. Here's . . . to Thacker!"

"To Thacker!"

The ice clunks off my teeth as the malt puts fire in my belly and water in my eyes.

"Puts fucking hairs on your chest that bad boy, eh?" Dennis slams down the glass, one of the ice cubes almost jumping out onto the table.

"Sure does. Lovely stuff though. Really, really nice," I say, looking at my empty glass, nodding.

"Speaking of hair, Hunter." Dennis gets up and walks back to the kitchen area. "I'm afraid we're going to have to do something about yours."

"Oh?"

"Yeah." He pops the corked lid off the bottle of Highland Park. "You see, when you were doing your audition, the only thing that wasn't quite right was your hair." He pours more into the glasses and looks over. "That wavy, untidy look hasn't been in fashion for years, if at all. Don't get me wrong, it suits you okay, you pull it off, but I just don't see Thacker looking like Hugh Fearnley-Whittingstall minus the glasses."

I run a hand through my ringlets. He places the whisky in front of me and sits down. "That's okay, I understand. So what kind of hair do you think Thacker should have then?"

"I was thinking really short. A top detective with a drug habit isn't going to bother with maintaining long hair. Know what I mean?"

"Yeah, it's no problem. I'll get myself a set of clippers and give it maybe a gauge four or something. That sound about right?"

"Perfect!" He raises his glass. "Here's to a short-haired Thacker!"

I look at my glass and exhale like I'm half-heartedly blowing out candles on a birthday cake.

"What's wrong? I assumed you wanted another because you said it was 'really, really nice'," he says, using air quotes. "I didn't think I had to ask if you wanted another one." He leans over, looks into my eyes then down at the glass. "Don't you want it?"

"I just don't want to get drunk. I can feel those two taking their–"

"To a short-haired Thacker!" Dennis blares, glass in the air.

"To a short-haired Thacker." And down they go.

Dennis looks at the ceiling and cheers. The sound, bouncing off the plastic ceiling, makes me jolt, followed instantly by laughter at the ridiculousness of getting a fright in a caravan with only two people in it.

"Really, really nice, Hunter, eh?" He reaches over and pats my shoulder. "Really, really, reeeeally nice. So tell me, are you married? Do you have children? What is it you do when you're not acting?"

"Eh, yeah, married to Celia, I have a son, Michael, and when I'm not acting I work part time as a surveyor. What about yourself?"

Through the window, I see the lights of an approaching car.

"Ah, here we go," Dennis says. "Not quite as noisy an arrival as you, eh?" He gets up from the table and starts dancing. "*Shake your money maker! Shake your money maker!*" I laugh. It should be awkward, but his dad-dancing is genuinely amusing.

The engine cuts and I hear the car door open and close, followed by the bleep of remote central locking.

"*Shake your money maker! Shake your money maker!* Fucking love Fleetwood Mac! You've got good taste, Hunter, my boy!"

The knock on the door goes 1-2-3, 1-2-3, 1-2-3-4-5-6-7.

"Mr Fleming, come on in. Looking the part, sir, looking the part."

For a split second, I think Mr Fleming is Adidas, but I quickly realise it's a police officer's uniform I'm looking at, not a black and white sports top.

"Hunter, this is Archer Fleming. Archer, Hunter Carr."

I stand and put out a hand, feeling a little drunk. "Nice to meet you."

"Likewise." He gives my hand a firm shake and smiles.

"Archer is playing Thacker's colleague, Clive Randall," Dennis says.

"Ah, excellent," I say, sounding a bit like Hugh Grant in *Four Weddings and a Funeral*.

"Can I interest you in a single malt, Archer?"

"Dennis, you know me well enough to know that I take these things seriously. Clive Randall wouldn't drink on the job, so the same applies to me . . . We *are* having a read-through, aren't we? Please tell me I didn't come in costume for nothing."

"No, no, you're right, we're definitely having a read-through," Dennis says, putting the bottle of Highland Park into a cupboard, next to what looks like a box of tea bags.

"If I drink, I might not be able to perform to the best of my abilities."

"You're quite right, Archer, and I admire your dedication to the cause. Quite the professional isn't he, Hunter?"

"Yes," I nod, meekly. "Dennis, could I maybe have a cup of tea if you've got any, please?"

"I can give you water?"

"Sure, water's fine."

"Water will be fine for me too," Archer says.

"Three waters coming up. Please, Archer, have a seat."

Archer sits across from me, where Dennis was before he got up to dance. "Brilliant script, isn't it?"

"It's excellent. The characters are three-dimensional and well thought through and the plot is juicy. It's a winning combination," I smile.

Archer leans over the table slightly, turning his shoulder away from Dennis. "I know, I wrote a bit of it."

"Oh, really, which bit?"

"The bit about the sandwich shop being the shop front for Thacker's ching." He taps his nose twice and sniffs.

"There we are, three glasses of H_2O to lubricate the vocal chords," Dennis says, placing the glasses on the table.

"You know they're actually called vocal *folds*, not chords," Archer says as Dennis sits down next to him.

"That's really interesting," Dennis says, glaring at him until he looks away.

"Dennis, see just before we get started," I say. "Is it okay if I give my wife a quick call, just to let her know I won't be home until tom–"

"You won't be able to. There's no reception out here. You can walk down to the road once we've had a read-through, or if you ask Archer nicely, he might give you a lift. It'll probably be dark once we're done." He glances out the window at the night drawing in. It's at that stage where it looks like the air's thick with dirt.

"Shall we get started then?" Archer says.

"Yes, let's start with you, Hunter," Dennis points. "As you know, I thought your audition was amazing – absolutely outstanding – so we know you clearly understood and appreciated everything that was going on in that scene. But, just so we're 100% on the same page, give us a quick synopsis of the story so we know you fully understand and appreciate the complexities of Thacker as a character. Because – and I've said this many times before – if we nail this, I think it could be as big as *Cracker*, *The Wire*, *24*, *Breaking Bad*, if not bigger. We need something to compete with all the good stuff that's coming out of the States. And I think this is it."

I take a mouthful of water and rest my forearms on the table. "Thacker is a detective investigating a string of bank and art gallery robberies and has a functioning addiction to cocaine. It's a complicated case which becomes his life, so he needs more cocaine to fuel his concentration and take the edge off his stress. He gets his daily fix from Donald Fox, who runs a sandwich shop. Fox hides bags of cocaine in paninis and sells them to his clients, over the counter under the noses of the lunching general public."

"Why are you slurring your words?" Archer asks, frowning slightly.

"Am I? I didn't realise I was."

"Carry on," Dennis says.

I take another mouthful of water. "Okay, so as the case becomes more intense, Thacker asks Fox for more cocaine, but he says no because he doesn't want things to get too . . . big."

"Too big?" Archer says, slowly sipping his water.

"Fox sells narcotics to a handful of reliable, regular customers who have professional lives and that suits him fine," I continue, unfazed. "It's a nice little money spinner for him, which, coupled with his sandwich shop, allows him to enjoy a good standard of life. He has no desire to be the Scarface or Heisenberg of the town. Thacker, however, won't accept this and, using his knowledge of security systems, breaks into the shop, steals every panini containing cocaine and finds the remainder of the stash. Fox, with his suspicions and now a cocaine-free shop, reports the break-in and requests a full enquiry. The case is given to Clive Randall, who's been assisting Thacker with his investigations."

I hold up four fingers. "Thacker therefore has:

One: an indefinite supply of cocaine, which may or may not see him to the end of the robbery case,

Two: a supplier that suspects him of theft,

Three: the possibility of his colleagues questioning him about it, and

Four: an agonising moral conflict whereby he's breaking

more laws than he's upholding, despite his professionalism and dedication to the cause."

"Why can't he just get cocaine somewhere else?" Dennis asks.

"Because Fox's product is top drawer. Best in the country. And the shop arrangement was perfect for him. Dealing with other dealers and making transactions under bridges or in dodgy clubs is something Thacker doesn't want to do, nor has the time for. He's got to be on the ball with the robbery case because he wants to get promoted. It's a classic 'who am I, what have I become?' story. Thacker is constantly questioning his own decision-making and while he has many strengths, he knows it's his weaknesses that drive him. This makes the character ideal for the writers to take him into a second series. You can do anything with that, really, don't you think? I mean, in this script, there's no mention of his sexuality, if he has a wife or partner. You could also–"

"That's fine, you can stop there, Hunter. Okay, I'm happy with that. You've certainly got a grasp of what we're trying to do here, which, after your audition, I was expecting anyway. Archer?"

"All sounds good to me." He sifts through a couple of sheets of paper, looks at Dennis, at me, back to the paper, then back to Dennis. We simultaneously sip water.

"What do you think of Dustin Hoffman?" Dennis asks.

"Dustin Hoffman?"

"*Tootsie*, *The Graduate*, *Straw Dogs*, *Rain Man*."

"Yeah, yeah, I know who you mean."

"What do you think of him?"

"What do you think of him?" Archer repeats.

"Well, I think he's very good. *Rain Man* is one of my favourite films."

"I'm an excellent driver," Archer stammers, and we all laugh.

"Never mind *Rain Man* though, have you seen *Marathon Man*?" Dennis asks.

"No. I don't think so anyway."

"You would remember," Archer says. "It's not a film people forget easily."

"Thomas 'Babe' Levy – what a performance!" Dennis says. "We think Hoffman is one of the living greats. I can't think of a bad film he's been in."

"Even *Meet the Fockers*?" I say.

Dennis and Archer look like I've just told them that their wives are playing away from home.

"Bad film rather than bad performance," Dennis says, dismissively. "Anyway, one of the reasons Hoffman's so convincing on screen is because of his dedication to method acting. There's a scene in *Marathon Man* where Babe Levy hasn't slept for three nights straight, so what did Hoffman do? He stayed up for three nights so he could truly feel his character's pain, his emotions, his complete exhaustion. Now that's what I call dedication to the cause, don't you think?"

"Fffff, that is impressive," I say.

Archer pops the studs on one of the pockets of his police officer's vest and pulls out a pouch of white powder. "Yes. Yes, it is."

"Have you snorted cocaine before, Hunter?" Dennis raises an eyebrow.

"Eh, no, never. I'm pretty much anti-drugs, guys."

There's an awkward silence. As they look from me to each other, I shift in my seat, killing the silence with the sound of trouser linen and vinyl cushion coming together.

Dennis rubs the back of his head with his hand, takes off his glasses and leans forward.

"We might have a problem here, Hunter. I mean, how the fuck are you going to be able to get under the skin of Thacker if you've never taken a line of ching before? The guy's out his tits on it for about 90% of the bastard story."

"Well, what about my audition? I was so good, you gave me the part there and then, and sent everyone home. That was a scene between Thacker and Fox where Thacker was on it."

"I didn't think this would be a problem." Dennis hits his fingertips off the edge of the table. "When you pulled up here, you were listening to Fleetwood Mac at full blast. Fleetwood fucking Mac! Back when they were brilliant! *Shake your money maker!* And why were they brilliant? 'Cos they were out their fucking tits the whole time! And don't tell me a whacko like Hugh Fearnley-Whittingstall hasn't had a line or two!"

"I'm not actually a Hugh Fearnley-Whittingstall fan. I just kinda look like him," I mutter, head in my hands, "but without the glasses."

Archer shifts the papers, empties the powder onto the table and pulls his wallet from his trouser pocket. "Why don't you just try it?" He takes out a £20 note and a credit card and begins separating the cocaine into lines.

Dennis gets up and walks across to the fridge. "If I'd picked that smelly guy with the Motorhead jacket, I bet he wouldn't have a problem snorting free ching. He'd happily get closer to fully understanding his character." He throws his arms around like a child building up to a tantrum then takes a Heineken from the fridge, pulls the ring and guzzles.

"Now's probably the best time to tell you, Hunter,"

Archer says, not looking at me, his full concentration on preparing the cocaine.

"Tell me what?"

"That there's someone else in the running for Thacker."

I feel my heart beat in my chest. I've already had the celebratory champagne dinner with Celia and Michael. My agent has posted it on her website. It's on Facebook, Twitter and LinkedIn. Michael's told people at college that his dad's going to be on the telly. Every man and his dog in our street know, including the ice-cream man.

"Sorry, what?" I gulp.

Dennis finishes his beer, scrunches the can and throws it onto the worktop. "There was a guy a couple of hours before you who was first class. We were going to call it a day there and then, but decided it would be unfair as he was only the fourth to audition."

"What, and he's *still* in the running? Is this a wind-up?"

"I'm afraid not," Archer says, rolling the £20 note.

Dennis faces the table, hands on hips. "The difference is, we didn't tell him he had the part."

"But we did tell him he had a very good chance." Archer presents Dennis with the note.

"We're going to make a final decision after we've had a read-through with both of you. He's coming here later in the week." Dennis takes the note, sits down and snorts a line. "Oooooooo yeaaaaaaah!"

I'm going to look like a total idiot if I have to go back and tell everyone I actually *don't* have the part. "Well, what is he like?"

"It would be unethical to tell you, Hunter, but he's different," Archer says. Dennis nods, rubbing residue into his gums.

"Different? Different how?"

"Well, he looks nothing like Hugh Fearnley-Whittingstall."

"And we know from his agent that he's a method actor," Dennis adds.

I think about Michael and how excited he was when he heard. He had said he wanted to come and watch me on set one day, meet the other actors and the director, get them to sign his autograph book.

"Right, give me that note." I close my eyes and do it really quickly. I sit back and splutter, and even though I didn't manage the whole line, I did it. I did it.

"That's my boy!" Dennis laughs. "Now let's get reading!"

"Are you not having any?" I ask Archer, sniffing and rubbing my nose, feeling the instant onset of euphoria.

"No. Clive Randall is an upstanding officer of the law, and actually, so am I." Archer slams his police badge onto the table in front of me. "Hunter Carr, I'm arresting you for the consumption of narcotics in the presence of a police officer. You have the right to remain silent. Anything you say can, and will, be used against you in a court of law. You have the right to talk to a lawyer and—"

"You must be joking! Is this for real? You're actually a police officer?"

"I said you have the right to remain silent!" Archer roars, stunning me to silence. He stands up and pulls out a pair of handcuffs. Still high, I don't struggle. Dennis looks at me and shrugs. I stand up and let Archer cuff me.

"Sit down," he says.

We sit in unison.

"Your son, Michael," Dennis says, waving a finger.

"What about him?"

"Who said you could speak?" Archer snarls.

"Let him speak," says Dennis.

"What about him? What about Michael? What the hell is all this ab–?"

"He raped my daughter, that's what!" Dennis jumps to his feet, face purple with rage, body arced like a pirate's cutlass. "My poor Roseanna is in pieces; she's a fucking wreck! She fell for the charms of that cunt of a son of yours and was lured to a basement flat where she was fucked three times against her will!" The words catch in his throat, the veins around his temples protruding like they're trying to jump out his head. He lifts a hand to his mouth and turns away.

I sit still but my heart is pounding hard as I absorb what I've just heard. Archer gets up and walks towards the sink, back turned. Dennis's muffled sobs break the silence. Self-hatred burns in my gullet as, fighting back my own tears, I struggle to accept that my son could be capable of such an atrocity. He was a problem child, always whining, seeking attention and tormenting other kids. Then at high school he got in with a bad crowd, started taking drugs. Celia and I had the police at the door a few times, once because he was involved in robbing a pub. I thought he had settled down a little bit, especially since he'd got a place at university, but this? My son? A rapist? I'll fucking kill him.

"So *that's* why I'm here?" I ask, unable to wipe away my tears.

"Archer, the gun, please," Dennis says.

Archer pulls open a drawer, lifts out a revolver and throws it to Dennis, who releases the safety and points it in my face.

"Whoa whoa whoa whoa, what the fuck?" I look into the barrel of the gun, Dennis's blurry contorted face behind it.

"Nobody fucks with my daughter! NOBODY!"

I close my eyes and think about what I want my final thought to be.

"But the good news, Hunter," Dennis says, calmly clicking the safety back on, "is that I'm not going to shoot you." He sits down and rests the gun on the table. "You're going to be the shooter."

"I'm not shooting my son!"

"I'm not asking you to shoot your son. Stop making assumptions. Thacker would never do that, would he, Archer?"

"No, of course not," Archer says, re-joining us at the table.

"We want you to live on the other side of the law, Hunter," Dennis continues. "We want you to wear Thacker's skin. See with his eyes. Breathe air into his lungs. That's what Hoffman would do, and just look at the career he's marked out for himself."

"I don't understand. Are you telling me that–"

"Look, I know *you* didn't rape my daughter, but you're the one who needs to make amends, my friend. It's perfect really. Even though you look like Hugh Fearnley-Whittingstall, we still want you to play Thacker–"

"Unless the other guy is better," Archer interrupts.

"Yes, thank you, Archer. Thing is, Hunter, we know you're brilliant. And you know you're brilliant."

"I'm not killing anyone," I say.

"Who said killing? There you go again."

"Making assumptions," Archer says. "You're not doing yourself any favours here."

Dennis leans forward. "Archer here has a lead on a local drug dealer and has reason to believe that Michael got some gear from him for the very party he and my daught . . ." He looks down, covering his face with his hands.

"We want you to find him and shoot him," Archer says.

"If he dies, fine, but a bullet to the shoulder or knee will do."

"And then what? You expect me to play Thacker?"

Dennis removes his hands from his face and looks up. "If you still want to, yes."

". . ."

"And obviously your narcotics charge will be dropped." Archer nods.

". . ."

". . ."

I look at the ceiling. "Okay, I'll do it."

Dennis bursts out laughing. "We're only kidding, Hunter! You see, fuck Dustin Hoffman and his method acting! When he turned up on set looking totally knackered, Lawrence Olivier said to him 'try acting, dear boy'. That's fucking brilliant, eh?" Dennis wipes tears from his eyes, Archer guffawing next to him, his shoulders bouncing up and down. "That wasn't even cocaine! You're high on flour and bicarbonate of soda! Ha ha ha ha!"

I look down at the white residue on the table and somehow manage a smile.

"I honestly couldn't give a fuck who my daughter sees," Dennis continues, dabbing his brow with a tissue, "she's a little slut anyway."

As Archer leans over to remove the cuffs, my smile breaks into a laugh.

"Hunter, why would I call my daughter a slut?" Dennis asks, all signs of laughter suddenly gone. "If you had a daughter, would you call her a slut? Would you find it funny if you knew three guys were sitting in a caravan laughing their heads off at how much of a big cum-gargling whore she is? Eh?"

Their expressions imply there hasn't been laugher in this caravan all year, let alone only seconds ago.

"Well, no." I say.

Dennis explodes into a fit of laughter again, and then, just as quickly, his expression is deadpan, like someone's flicked a switch. "But no, really?"

"Now that's what I call acting, dear boy," Archer says, and the laughter returns.

"Well done, Hunter, you're thick-skinned, I'll give you that. Okay, you bought that your son's a rapist and that you'd snorted cocaine, but you made the right decision when your life was at stake, didn't you? That's just what we need for Thacker, my man, just what we need! I think you and I are going to get on just fine!" He bursts out laughing again. "Aw, man, that was priceless, I need another whisky. Would you care to join me, dear boy?"

I take a deep breath. "No, not just now. Maybe after the reading."

"Archer?"

Archer gets up. "Just water for me," he says, walking past Dennis to the toilet.

"Do Michael and your daughter actually know each other?" I ask, "Or was that just made up too?"

"They went out on a couple of dates," Dennis says from behind the door of the cupboard he put the whisky in. "But they decided to just be friends. She said he was a nice guy, but there was just no chemistry."

"A nice guy," I repeat, softly.

"Right, what about this reading then?" Archer asks. "Shall we get started?"

Dennis puts a dash of water in his whisky and then fills a glass for Archer. When they're back at the table, Dennis plucks excerpts of the script from the pile of papers. "Okay, I'll read Fox, but let's start with the Thacker monologue in the scene between Thacker and Randall. Hunter, this is your opportunity to convince us that the only person to play *The Panini Thief* is you." He holds my gaze for a few seconds then sits down. "Okay, go."

"And don't slur your words," Archer says.

I throw the script to the floor, hard so it flutters.

"Did you really think I thought that was cocaine?" I ask, smiling.

Dennis and Archer look at each other and laugh. Under the table, one wrist resting on the gun in my pocket, I rub my thumbs up and down the recesses between my index and middle fingers, and begin.

Time to Begin

As she walks towards the church, Nikita focuses on the sound of birdsong. She's fed up hearing the words 'I'm so sorry for your loss' but knows she'll hear them again countless times before the day expires. The slight chill in the spring air is affecting her breathing, but she does her best to draw as little attention as possible to her short, sharp breaths. In silhouette above the church, a flock of birds dance in the vastness of an azure sky. Nikita is mesmerized by their hypnotic energy, how they change direction so suddenly, yet majestically, as if their movements have been expertly choreographed.

"Nikita, darling, I just want to say how sorry I am for your loss," Auntie Marjorie says, gripping her arm tightly, as if Nikita was, at any moment, going to lose her balance and topple to the ground. "What a terrible thing to happen! And listen, if there's anything I can do, don't hesitate to ask, okay?"

"I'll be okay, Auntie Marjorie." Nikita pats her aunt's arm with her opposite hand.

" . . . "

"Look at the birds up there. Amazing, aren't they?"

"Yes, dear."

"That's what Paul was, you know – a creature of the skies. Never happier than when he knew he was going skydiving. He used to say to me that I should take it up too, so we could go on skydiving holidays together and see the world's landmarks from a bird's eye view."

"Is that right, dear?" Auntie Marjorie is now stroking Nikita's arm as if it's a dog.

"You should look up some of his videos on YouTube. The views on his parachute-cam are awesome. You know, I would've been up for giving it a try if it wasn't for the little fact that I'm scared of heights," Nikita laughs.

"Yes, dear, probably not the best of hobbies for someone like you," Auntie Marjorie smiles, continuing to stroke her arm. She knew not to use the word vertigo. Nikita preferred 'scared of heights'. It sounded less official, as if it could be cured, or that she'd one day get over it.

Before the service starts, another three people – Auntie Hannah and two of Paul's pals – tell Nikita that they're sorry for her loss and offer their help. Nikita sits next to her parents during the service, her mother's hand on top of hers, fingers interlocked. Paul's mother gets up and says a few words about her son, but she has to cut it short. It's such an emotionally-charged moment that most of the congregation has to wipe tears from their eyes. Paul's sister, Carlie, howls. Nikita keeps it together, her eyes dry, concentrating on her breathing.

At the wake, partly because there's alcohol, people hug each other. With bottles of beer in their hands, a group of Paul's friends from the skydiving club huddle together gracelessly, arms around necks, ties loosened, singing out of tune Britpop songs. After many awkward conversations and hugs, Nikita finally manages to finish her first glass of wine and heads to the buffet for a refill. While she's there, one of the hotel's catering staff brings out a smooth, dark brown, dome-shaped cake and places it at the end of the table.

"What is that?" Nikita asks.

"Refrigerator cake," the girl says.

"Refrigerator cake? What does that . . . mean?"

"It just means it has to be kept in the fridge. Well, you can take it out of the fridge, obvos," she laughs, "but if it doesn't get eaten, or put back *in* the fridge, it begins to sort of shrink and fall apart."

"Oh."

"Grab yourself a plate. You can have the first slice."

Nikita picks up a plate from the other end of the buffet table as the girl plunges a knife into the heart of the cake.

"There you go." The girl lifts a generous slice onto her plate. "And I take it you're after a refill too? White is it?"

"Oh, yes, please." Nikita examines the slice. "A cake you have to look after, eh?"

"Yip. If it was up to me, I'd call it TLC cake. If you look after it, it looks after you."

"Eh? It looks after you?" Nikita says, quizzically.

"Yeah, 'cos it tastes gorgeous," she laughs. "Go on, try it."

Nikita takes a bite of the cool, soft, succulent cake.

"Your face just lit up," the girl grins.

"Bloody hell, that is gorgeous! It kind of reminds me of tiffin . . . oh, and Christmas cake too, only less rich."

"Have a look online, you'll get plenty recipes there. That one's apricot, raisin and pecan, but there are loads of variations."

"Mmmm, thanks, I will." Nikita takes another bite, looking round to see if anyone's watching.

"Don't forget your wine."

"Oh, yeah, thanks."

Nikita places her glass on a nearby table and hopes she can take a few moments to herself to finish her slice of refrigerator cake. But with her cheeks bulging from the last bite, she sees Carlie emerge from the crowd and totter towards her with open arms and wine-blackened lips.

"Nikita, honey, come here," she bubbles, her face like a mother consoling her toddler after a banged head. She squeezes hard, running her hands down Nikita's hair, the occasional strand being caught by a scraggly nail. "We'll be okay, honey, we'll be okay. We can help each other through this."

Nikita's jaws work hard to break down the refrigerator cake. As Carlie continues to squeeze, Nikita makes sure her mouth is firmly closed, conscious of the possibility of inhaling one of her wavy golden locks or refrigerator cake being squeezed onto the back of her jacket.

When Carlie finally stops, Nikita swallows the last of the cake and looks into her eyes. She sees resemblance to Paul and her eyes flood with tears.

"That's it Nikita, honey, you let it all out, you let it all out, there, there, honey, that's it, that's it, it's good to grieve. Oh God, look, you've got me started again too. Oh, come here you."

"No, Carlie, no!" Nikita holds up her hands. A few people look round, including Nikita's parents. "Just give me some time to myself, okay?"

"Darling, are you alright?" her mother asks. "Is there anything we can do?"

"I'm fine, Mum, I'm fine! I just need some time to myself, okay? Just . . . just give me a bit of time." Sobbing deep, shaky sobs, she picks up her glass, power walks out of the hotel and makes her way along the farm road towards the river.

Once there, she sits on the riverbank and just listens to the sounds of wildlife, pleased to see no-one around. The spring breeze has dried her tears on her face, leaving defined tracks. She finishes her wine and rests her glass on the grass. The sky is still azure and clear, bar a few fluffy, picture-book clouds. The sun reflects off the surface of the river, whose continuous flow is satisfying against the stillness and greenness of the riverbank and permanence of the river birches and weeping willows.

Nikita clocks some movement in nearby vegetation. Curious as to what's there, she fixes her gaze, her mind occasionally playing tricks on her, making things move when they haven't. And then, despite blinking several times, she sees the whiskers and nose of an otter poking out of its holt. It pops in and out, showing no more of its face, assessing its environment for danger. When it disappears, Nikita waits, hoping it'll come out again. She doesn't want to move in case she scares it, so she sits patiently and quietly, her mind focused on keeping her breathing inaudible, helped by the backing track of birdsong and distant barking. And then, just as she is considering giving up, the otter appears, accompanied by a cub who seems reluctant to take to the water. But with a bit of encouragement from its mother the cub soon accustoms itself and they swim downstream together. And although it's all over in seconds, Nikita feels privileged to have witnessed the apprehension and excitement of new life experiencing new adventure.

Her tears begin to flow again. She lifts up her blouse and examines her cracked ribs and bruised torso, still aching from Carlie's hug. Underneath her bra she can still feel the pain of his bite. Of course, her face was always fine so she could go out in public. Paul knew what he was doing. He claimed her shortness of breath was because she had been clearing the loft and was exposed to a lot of dust.

Nikita never found out why he did it; why he kept doing it. For a while she blamed her vertigo 'cos it prevented her from jumping out of planes with him, but there had to be something deeper. At least she hoped there was. But any time she asked, to try and help him, he lashed out.

Crying only aggravates her injuries, so she closes her eyes, straightens her back and concentrates on calming down. To the sounds of a chiff-chaff chorus, she breathes the fresh country air in through her nose and out through her mouth, meditating her way back to normality. When she opens her eyes, she looks into the river and thinks she catches a glimpse of the otter cub, but it's probably her mind playing tricks on her again. Squinting a little against the sun, she gazes up at the sky and thinks about Paul jumping into it at 10,000 feet, and the panic on his face when he deployed his parachute and his frayed lines snapped, thanks to her penknife.

She looks at the river tumbling and burbling with momentum, breathing and hissing, carrying its habitat in one direction, and feels lucky to be alive.

"Time to begin," she announces to the nature around her, smiling through the pain. She picks up her empty wine glass, carefully levers herself to her feet and makes her way back to the hotel.

Woodland Berry

"Are you okay there? Can I help you with anything?"

"Eh . . . I'm just looking for a lipstick for my girlfriend's birthday . . . but it's difficult to know where to start." You glance at the floor and then at her name badge. Next to the Boots logo is the name Polly, engraved in black ink.

"Okay, well, what's her skin tone like? Does she wear a lot of foundation?" You look at her yellow face and can't help thinking of *The Simpsons*.

"Eh . . . only a little . . . and I'd say her skin tone is probably about the same as mine."

"Okaaaay." Polly scans the wall of colours. "How about we try . . . Woodland Berry from Estée Lauder? It's one of the pricier ones, but it is her birthday after all, isn't it?"

"Well, yeah, I suppose."

"Can I try a little bit of this on your hand to see how it looks next to your skin?" she asks, brandishing the lipstick.

"Eh . . . yeah, sure." She takes your hand in hers, striplights reflecting in her perfectly applied nail varnish.

"I'm not really meant to do this." She looks over her shoulders. "But if you're going to spend over twenty quid on a lipstick, you want it to be right, don't you?"

"Well . . . eh . . . well, yeah . . . yeah, of course." You start to sweat.

"It's a nice deep pink," she says, applying a line just below your thumb. Her touch is gentle and you enjoy feeling her skin next to yours.

"That's fine . . . yeah, that's fine. That looks good, I'll take it." You pull your hand away before it sweats onto hers.

"Well, that was a quick decision! I didn't think I was *that* good a salesperson," she laughs, twisting the stick and snapping the lid back on.

"Yeah, well, I can just picture it on her, though. It'll be perfect. Thanks very much."

"You're welcome." She hands you the lipstick with a head-tilted smile.

When you get home, you take a suitcase from the hall cupboard into your room. You place it on your bed and remove the lipstick from your pocket, the small plastic bag rustling. You rotate the indented wheels on the suitcase until the numbers display your code.

In the suitcase is a pair of indigo five-inch high-heeled ankle books with a suede finish by Even & Odd; Disco Pink Glossfinity nail polish and nail polish remover by Max Factor; Match Perfection Compact Powder and Lasting Finish Soft Colour Mono Blush by Rimmel London; Elnett Satin Hairspray by L'Oréal Paris; black fishnet stockings by Lovehoney; a black short skirt, pleated, by Missguided and a jewel-studded purple blouse by Punkyfish.

Once you've put on the fishnets, skirt and blouse, you make your way to the bathroom with the make-up. You lock the door, even though you live alone. With a wet comb, you make a side parting in your hair and, using the Elnett Satin Hairspray, you do your best to style it like Emma Watson's, or Winona Ryder's when her hair was short. After a bit of trial and error, you manage to get it into a shape you're happy with.

You take your time with the make-up, like a portrait painter with great attention to detail. You get the foundation right first time, but apply too much blusher which makes you look like a clown or a hooker, so you have to wash the whole lot off and start again. Second time round it's not perfect, but it's a marked improvement, the blusher accentuating your naturally high cheekbones, a feature many girls have commented on – with envy. After you carefully apply the Disco Pink nail polish, gagging slightly on the fumes, it's time for the finishing touch.

Once your lips are coated with the deep, sensual colour of Woodland Berry, you turn your shoulders and pout. You laugh, throwing back your head, and when you look back at your reflection, you love seeing your smile outlined by such a stimulating, glamorous colour; a frame of sexiness and fun, an allure that perfectly matches your skin tone and compliments your scintillating personality.

You strike some poses: hands behind your head, sticking out an imaginary bust; hands clasped together like a gun – a Charlie's Angel shooting at the camera; the pondering misunderstood artist; the sophisticated film star; the winner of the beauty pageant.

You walk back to your room and put on the indigo ankle boots. When you stand, you're uneasy at first, but after walking from room to room your confidence builds and you begin to strut, your calf muscles taut with new responsibility. Hands on hips, jutting your right hip out as much as you can – to take away your straightness – you examine yourself in your full-length mirrored wardrobe. You're annoyed at forgetting to buy eyeliner and mascara, but you still feel quite sexy, even though you can see long, frizzy brown hairs poking through your fishnets. As you adjust your position to minimise their visibility, your landline rings. You sit on your bed, cross your legs and pick up the receiver.

"Hello?"

"Gary, man, it's Panda."

"Alright, man, how's it going?"

"Sound, man. S'happening?"

"Nothing much." You smile at your reflection. "Just chilling."

"Cool. So, listen, are you alright for the five-a-sides this week? I want to get the same team as last week if I can, man, 'cos I thought we played really well together. That was some goal you scored, by the way, mind the volley? That was amazing, man!"

"Aw, cheers, man, and yeah, I'm up for it. Same time as last week?"

"Sound, man. Yeah, same time."

"Cool. So, is that you got everybody now? Or am I the first?" You stroke the suede on the heel of your boot with your free hand.

"Just Big Jason to go, man. I'm going to give him a phone the now. But even if he can't make it, wee Joe'll fill in and we'll still win again, man. Defo."

"Nice one, sir."

"Sound, Gary, man. Right, I'll see you on Thursday."

"Okay, man, cheers, bye."

You just wanted to know how it'd feel to be like a girl. And although you look a bit silly, you like it. You really like it. You're not interested in men, though. In fact, the thought of a man wanting to do anything sexual to you makes you feel, well, a bit queasy. But you would like to be more glamorous; to have more choice when it comes to getting dressed up. But if you went out like this, you'd be labelled a freak; called a poof. And if you shaved your legs, the guys at the five-a-sides would slaughter you for being a weirdo. And even if you told them you weren't gay and that they were 'safe', well, they probably wouldn't believe you and it'd be no surprise if your place on the team was given to someone else, your talent for a long-distance volley suddenly unimportant.

You sit on your bed, flip open your laptop and log onto eBay. You look up eye liner, mascara, leggings, frilly knickers and knee-high boots, looking occasionally at your reflection, picturing how they would look on you.

When your doorbell rings, you freeze. It rings again, followed by a friendly knock on the door. Then the letterbox opens.

"Hello, son, it's just us, we just thought we'd pop by. We've got that painting for you for your bedroom – the one of your Uncle Frank's we've had up the loft. We would've phoned but we went and left our blooming mobiles at home. Are you there, son?"

"He must be in, his car's in the drive," your dad says. "He's maybe just got headphones on or something. Just give the door a quick try, Carol."

"Oh, he *is* in . . . Hello, dear, it's just us! We've got that painting for you. Are you there, Gary? . . . Gary?"

Type

When her message appears on the screen, I frantically scan for the words I want to see. I sit back, read again and absorb them slowly. Prickly heat distorts my arms and I rub them gently, first the right with my left hand then the left with my right. Horace pads out of the kitchen without even a glance in my direction. He lies in the centre of the room and begins to wash. Wish I had got a dog instead.

I minimise her message, open a new session and go into my profile. I click on the photo and examine my physique and expression.

> *I mean, the topless photo tells me*
> *you're only after one thing.*

I just wanted to display my achievement. In every other photo I'm fully clothed and smiling, sometimes with friends around me.

I thought girls would want me to be toned.

I go to her profile and feel the disappointment sink deeper. I click on her first photo and look into her deep brown eyes, still able to see the kindness that made me send her a message in the first place. Her long dark hair is naturally straight with some split ends and mild frizz, resting coolly on her mustard biker's jacket. Her undecorated lips outline a smile of untarnished teeth and, behind her on a stand, half cut out of the photo, is a burgundy Les Paul.

I want to take her to Glastonbury on the Fazer.

I click on another photo. No smile this time. She looks pensive; poetic. Cool and complex; beautiful in black and white.

You're
not
my type.

She could have lied and told me that she'd been on a couple of dates with someone else and that it was going really well. I'd still have been disappointed. But not hurt.

Horace miaows at the door so I let him out. He doesn't look up and quickly disappears over the wall. I close the door to hear only the whir of my computer. I sit down and look at her first photo again. Then click on Home.

Time to find someone who'll appreciate me. My Fazer. My timeshare in France. That I have emotions. Ambitions. And bitchin' dance moves.

Plastic Eyes

"Ryan, my friend, how are you?"

"Good, thanks, Mr Willis. How's yourself? Popular again, I see." I thumb over my shoulder at the queue.

"Better being busy than bored, son," he smiles. "Now, what'll it be this week? I've got deals on haddock, pollock and king prawns."

"Sold!" I scan the counter to see what else takes my fancy.

"Two of each, I take it?" Mr Willis says over his shoulder, lathering his hands in the sink.

"Yeah, more than two prawns, though," I laugh.

Mr Willis rolls his eyes, dries his hands and begins picking the fish.

"I'll have some lemon sole too, please . . . some . . . calamari . . . and . . . eh . . ."

Mr Willis leans over the counter. "I'll do you those trout half price if you want," he whispers.

I look at the trout. Their black eyes.

In all the years I've been coming here – every Wednesday afternoon – Mr Willis has never noticed that the fish I buy is nearly always boned and headless.

"Sure, that'd be great," I whisper back.

While he's picking, weighing and bagging, I overhear two women behind me:

"Did you hear about that poor drummer getting killed?" one says.

"Yes, shocking, isn't it? And he was a dad as well. Honestly, I don't know what this country's coming to."

"And how's Lydia?" Mr Willis asks.

"Yeah, she's fine, thanks. She's given me her old phone – it's one of those smart ones." I take the phone out of my pocket and raise it in the air as if Mr Willis wouldn't believe me if I didn't show him. "*'You need to get yourself into the 21ˢᵗ century,'* she said to me. I'm still kinda getting used to it to be honest."

"I thought a young man like you would be well in the know with all that fancy new-fangled stuff."

"I'm not actually that young, Mr Willis," I whisper. "I'm 41."

"Right, there we go, grandpa, that's you," he chuckles, plonking a large paper bag on the counter.

"Thanks. What's the damage?"

"£22.80."

I hand him £25.

"Thank you, my friend; I'll just get your change. You heading through to the city tonight, then? Or is it home to the pipe and slippers?"

"I'll leave that kind of thing to seniors like you," I laugh. "But yeah, I'll be heading through once I've stocked the freezer and fed the cat."

"Well, you enjoy yourself, son. And make sure you cook that calamari right, there's nowt worse than when it ends up like chewing gum."

"Don't you worry, Mr Willis, I'm an expert when it comes to cooking anything that lives in water. See you next week."

"Thanks again, Ryan, see you later . . . Yes, ladies, now, what can I do you for?"

When I get home I place the calamari in the fridge for

tomorrow night's dinner and the fish and prawns in the freezer. I give Freddy a big helping of Whiskas with tuna and then spend a bit of time stroking his coat and playing with his toy mouse, although he loses interest quickly and disappears through his flap and into the garden.

Upstairs, I empty my pockets onto the bed, take off my trousers and hang them in the wardrobe. My phone bleeps.

```
Hi gorjis mobbed at work today so
really lookin 4ward to date nite.
Starvin but tryin not 2 snack lol.
Hope ur getting to grips with ur
new phone ok. Btw u could get lucky
tonite C u 18r mwah Lx
```

Lydia's 40 but texts like a teenager. It's sweet though, we've still got our spark. And she loves fish as much as I do. When we first started dating, she took me to a small seafood restaurant in the city called *Seafarers' Delight*. I couldn't believe how small it was when we walked in – not much bigger than the average living room – but the food was sensational. We now go every Wednesday for a romantic meal because I finish early and Lydia works nearby.

```
I'll put on my best cologne ☺ See
you later x
```

I open Google and type in 'drummer death'. I wonder if it's someone famous like Chad Smith or Larry Mullen Jnr, killed in a random attack by a crazed fan, like the guy who shot John Lennon. I soon learn that a fusilier drummer was run over by Muslim extremists and hacked to death with a meat cleaver. It happened in Woolwich, shortly before 2.20pm, not long after I'd left work. The report cites British Military involvement in Afghanistan and other Muslim countries as the reason. They targeted him because he was wearing a Help for Heroes hoodie. I go into Facebook and click on my private group, 'The Lads'.

Reggie Cunningham Holy shit! What do yous make of that soldier getting killed?

Max Crow Bang out of order. Who the fuck do they think they are? What is wrong with this country?

Reggie Cunningham Cameron, man and the govt and forces fighting a war against terror, shoulder to shoulder wi the Americans, who sold them the arms in the first place

Max Crow Yeah but this didn't happen in Afghanistan or Iraq, it happened in Woolwich. In Britain! I mean WTF?

Reggie Cunningham They're Muslims though man, they did it cos British forces are going into the likes of Afghanistan an killing innocent people

Max Crow You saying the Brits are responsible for creating the terror like?

Reggie Cunningham Not necessarily. It's complicated

Max Crow It's complicated? Is that no what folk say about their relationship status? Its no quite the same as killing an innocent soldier on his own turf is it?

Reggie Cunningham Not excusing it, Maximo, just saying that we're part of a complex picture. Britain always sides with America, right? America goes into Muslim countries to dig for oil cos oil is power. They also sell arms to these countries or do deals in exchange for oil. Now understandably these countries are not happy cos a natural resource is being taken away from them, one that's important for economic stability/infrastructure etc so they use the arms to show their anger, hence 9/11, The Pentagon etc. And because we're America's little brother we get tarred with the same brush, even though we let in loads of immigrants and call ourselves a multicultural nation

Max Crow So we welcome immigrants with open arms, they come in, get a roof, use the NHS and then kill us. Great!

Reggie Cunningham The whole thing is flawed. It's all a big horrible power struggle. Some folk think 9/11 happened because of America's support for attacking Muslims in Somalia and Chechnya. Others think it was to do with Muslims trying to conquer the world, trying to take down the only country in their way of world domination: America. Like they weren't going to retaliate! I bet no-one thought something like this would happen though

Max Crow I've just read that the soldier's name was Lee Rigby, married but separated, with a two year old son.

Reggie Cunningham Man, that's grim

Max Crow Really grim. How do you explain this shit to a two-year-old? Sorry son, Daddy's been killed by Muslims because other people none of us know, who probably live in America, have killed Muslims in other countries.

Reggie Cunningham I know, it's terrible

Max Crow I mean, what do they think this is going to achieve eh? A fatherless son, a widow and lots of fucking angry people – yeah, that's really going to help settle things down isn't it? Fucking idiots. Why don't they fuck off back to where they belong?

Reggie Cunningham Cos the standard of living is better here. Remember what I said about the oil

Max Crow Fuck the oil! This has to be about more than oil. Are you telling me that all this war, fighting, hatred and KILLING innocent people boils down to just oil?

Reggie Cunningham It's a big part of it man, that's all I'm saying

Ryan Park Hi guys, just been reading this thread ☹

Reggie Cunningham What do you make of it all?

Ryan Park Are you guys ok?

Max Crow Yeah, course we are. Just debating.

Ryan Park It's horrible what's happened. I've got a Help for Heroes t-shirt, y'know

Reggie Cunningham Really?

Ryan Park Yeah, it could've been me

Max Crow Don't be fucking daft, Ryan, Woolwich is miles away, and how many Muslims do you know that live round here?

Ryan Park Theres a few actually and there are plenty in the city

Max Crow Yeah, but nowhere near as many as in London.

Reggie Cunningham How come you've got the t-shirt?

Ryan Park Bought it at a stand at the family day. Lydia thought it would be a nice thing to do

Reggie Cunningham Well, it was

Max Crow You've changed your tune.

Reggie Cunningham Eh? What you on about Max?

Max Crow Cos now you're saying that sending money to our injured troops, which indirectly supports the war, is a good thing. How can that possibly be a good thing? How come they're even called heroes if they're killing innocent Muslims?

Reggie Cunningham Oh come on, it's not like they go about looking for Muslims to kill. They do it in defence. They're actually there to prevent unrest and protect our country

Max Crow Yeah but based on what you said they shouldn't have to protect our country in the first place and they only have to cos there's no way back thanks to tossers like Blair siding with twats like Bush.

Reggie Cunningham Calm down Max

Max Crow No, I wont calm down Reggie! I've got family and friends in London. What if they get slayed as well, eh? Just cos they aren't Muslims.

Ryan Park Guys, let's just chill. A lot of this is just a reaction to what's happened today. It might not even be representing the facts accurately

Reggie Cunningham And you know all the facts do you, Ryan?

Ryan Park No, I'll be honest I don't. I just live in my own world sometimes, in fact most of the time

Max Crow That's the gaffer's van rolling in, I need 2 go. Speak l8r.

Ryan Park Ok, see you Max

Reggie Cunningham L8r mate

Ryan Park Not working today?

Reggie Cunningham Took a half day as need to go to the bank. Actually, I better get moving

Ryan Park No worries, maybe see you on Sunday afternoon for a pint?

Reggie Cunningham Yeah, maybe. Will need to check if Julie has anything in the calendar, but that sounds good

Ryan Park Cool, speak to you later

I click out of 'The Lads' and into my news feed. There are a lot of posts about what's happened. I click the red square to read private messages from my work colleague, Graeme, and Sharon, a girl I went to university with.

Graeme Porter Hey man, check this shit. Scandalous. Especially since the prick at the helm is the same man who thinks it's okay to leave his 8-year-old daughter in the pub and fight wars about fuck all. G

I click the link. It takes me to a Telegraph article from a few days ago – 'MPs could get £10,000 pay rise'. I glance at the photos of the bloated, pasty politicians but don't read the article.

Sharon Fergus Hi Ryan, check this. Thought you should be aware if you aren't already. If you use plastic bags, it's maybe time to stop! Shaz x

The link takes me to an article about fish - 'Over many years, a plastic soup has formed in our seas, caused by careless disposal of plastic bags and bottles. Thousands of marine animals choke and die from ingesting this plastic and many more are poisoned by the dioxins that emanate from this mass of plastic. Dioxins causes gender mutations in fish and land animals that eat fish, and if humans consume unsafe levels of dioxins, they can experience issues with fertility, as well as increasing their risk of cancer.'

I throw my phone to the other side of the bed as if it's responsible for everything and watch its illuminated screen fade to black. Sifting through the items in my wardrobe, I come across my Help for Heroes t-shirt. It has the strapline 'Support for our wounded'. I take it off its hanger, fold it and tuck it under a pile of bedsheets on the top shelf. I select my salmon-coloured shirt and blue corduroy jeans. I step into the jeans and place the shirt on the bed. My phone illuminates and I narrow my eyes at the piercing bleep.

```
Lol, excellent, sniff u 18r hunni
☺ xx
```

I drop the phone back onto the bed, chuckling. As I walk into the hall the phone bleeps again, but it's a different tone this time. I ignore it, go to the bathroom, take off my glasses, shave and then splash my face and neck with cologne. I then realise I haven't put in my contact lenses. I wash my hands twice before opening the case. I remove the left lens first and look in the mirror at my soft, smooth, clean face and slightly overgrown eyebrows. I look pretty serious so I smile, then let it fade slightly so I still look happy but with fewer wrinkles. After rinsing the lens in solution, I look at the ceiling, place it in my eye and blink until it focuses. Then I prise the right lens from the case, place it in the palm of my hand and soak it in solution.

"Plastic eyes", I say, examining it closely, carefully dragging little bits of eyelash and matter off it with my index finger.

I bring it closer to my eye. What a phenomenal piece of technology. A tiny piece of curved plastic tailored to my needs so I can see the world around me. Thanks to oil. I put it in my eye and watch my reflection become sharp and clear, which gives me a momentary buzz, as if a hangover has been lifted at the click of my fingers.

I funk up my hair with fancy expensive wax Lydia bought me, rinse my hands and walk back to the bedroom. I put on my shirt and give myself a nod in the mirror. My phone bleeps several times in a row as if it's just found a signal.

Joseph Campbell-Knox None of yous know what your talking about, 9/11 was government sponsored terrorism, end of. The Dubya-Bush regime ASSISTED it. Why? Two words, PEAK OIL. Without 9/11, America wouldn't have an excuse to invade Iraq and Afghanistan and take their oil, would they? Doing so gave the Americans a dominant military position right in the centre of the world's main oil production region so what you said about Muslims trying to conquer the world Reggie is a joke. Where did you get that shit from lol? So if yous want someone to blame for the death of that innocent drummer, you can point the finger at the American twat who reads books upside down!

Reggie Cunningham I wondered when you'd pipe up Joe. I can't actually remember where I got that from, probably a blog or something. But you can't say that Al-Qaeda aren't committed to the Quran and Sharia law so much that they kill to gain peace, can you?

Joseph Campbell-Knox Shite.   KILL to gain PEACE ??????

Reggie Cunningham So you don't think any of this has to do with religion and beliefs then?

Joseph Campbell-Knox You quite rightly said it's a power struggle but it's a power struggle about money and oil. Religion and terror are just the vehicles. It wouldn't make any difference if everyone in Iraq was a white Christian, Dubya-Bush would still have wanted his corrupt paws on their oil

Reggie Cunningham Shite

Joseph Campbell-Knox Well look at this country, it's proof that Muslims and British citizens of various religious beliefs can live in harmony

Reggie Cunningham Are you having a laugh Joe? Have you forgotten what happened today?

Joseph Campbell-Knox No Reggie I haven't but the point I'm making is that it wouldn't have happened if it wasn't for Dubya-Bush being a greedy power-mad oil-grabbing arsehole and 'Tory' Blair putting him on a fucking pedestal

Ryan Park It wouldn't have happened if he hadn't been wearing a Help for Heroes hoodie

I log out, slip the phone into the pocket of my jeans and head downstairs. I put on my leather jacket, check I've got everything and make my way to the railway station. My phone bleeps regularly and I fight the temptation to see what else has been said. I try to think about happier things, like going to Portugal in four weeks with Lydia and our friends Kim and Jason, but my mind drifts back to the soldier lying in the street in Woolwich, his heart no longer pumping.

Until now, I hadn't really noticed how many plastic bottles and take-away wrappers litter the streets leading to the railway station. When I arrive, an automated tannoy announcement informs me that the train is delayed by approximately eight minutes. A couple of young guys in hoodies shuffle up and down the platform cursing the rail company, smoking furiously. A well-dressed man carrying a briefcase looks at his phone. An Indian woman holds her young son's hand, occasionally looking down, smiling, saying things in her native tongue. I look at the debris people have thrown onto the track – juice bottles, tin cans, ice-cream wrappers, even milk cartons. Torn, discoloured plastic bags rustle in the branches of the overhanging trees as the train pulls up.

I walk up the carriage until I find a table I can sit at alone. My phone bleeps again. I think about switching it off but decide against it in case Lydia needs to get in touch. I glance around and everyone's looking at their phones, including the two hoodies and the Indian woman, whose son is leaning over, trying to see what's on her screen. I take mine out of my pocket.

> Hey gorjis Im here sipping a big yummy glass of wine ☺ how long u gonna b? Lxxx

Hi honey, train was delayed but
should be there in about 10mins.
Why not just order 4 me? Surprise
me. After all, it's not like I
don't like fish lol xxx

Lol ☺ Ok babes will do c u sn xxx

"Ooooooo, you smell nice," Lydia says with a flirty smile. I lean down and kiss her full on the lips. I take off my jacket and, as I hang it on the back of my chair, she pours me a glass of wine. I sit down and take a sip.

"Sauvignon Blanc? French?"

"One out of two. It's Italian."

"Mmmm, very nice." I take another sip and swirl it around in my mouth.

"How did you get on at Mr Willis's?" Lydia asks, head dipped, eyes looking up at me, the flame of the candle in the centre of the table reflecting in her pupils as she toys with her long blonde hair. I snigger.

"What?" She narrows her eyes and purses her lips.

"Nothing … It's just that I've never been asked before . . . well, in such a sexy way anyway . . . how my trip to the fishmongers was!"

She laughs, flicks her hair – narrowly missing the flame – and looks into my eyes, licking her lips. "So, big boy, what did you get? Tell me you got plaice, 'cos tonight I just might want to see … your plaice."

I nearly choke on my wine.

"Sorry, sweetheart, did you say something?" I lift my hand to my ear. "I'm afraid I'm a little hard of herring."

Once we stop giggling, I tell her what's in the freezer for the week and that it's calamari for tomorrow's dinner.

"Oh, but you'll obviously need to sort out the trout when we have it, okay?" I say.

"Sure, honey. In fact, speaking of which, I'll be doing a bit of that tonight … I've ordered us sea bass. Khushtar says it's to die for. Hey, speak of the devil."

"Hello, Ryan, trouble on the trains, my friend?" Khushtar says, extending his hand. Lydia's loveliness had distracted me, but now I was back thinking about it. What most of the country have been thinking and talking about since around 3 o'clock. And Lydia hasn't mentioned it. I think of Rigby's son, crying, asking when Daddy's coming home. And nobody knows what to say.

"Yeah, must've been a signalling problem or something," I say, shaking Khushtar's hand, his beard guiding my eyes to his familiar smile.

"You mean the guard didn't tell you over the tannoy? That's a bit poor, huh?"

"It's okay, I'm here now," I smile, but my mind isn't. 7/7; Rigby lying on the road; people looking out of office windows as the first plane approaches; bigger and bigger and bigger and bigger; upside-down book; SMASH; Blair's face morphing into Heath Ledger's Joker; Dubya-Bush on the golf course drinking oil from a crystal glass; *now watch this drive*; drive; drive into Rigby; Help for Heroes – Support for our wounded. My phone bleeps during the awkward silence. I release my grip. Khushtar withdraws his hand but maintains his smile. My hand is clammy so I run it down the side of my jeans.

"And that's the main thing, my friend," Khushtar says, doing an excellent job of pretending everything's normal. "You have your lovely lady sitting across from you, a glass of Italian white wine and the most magnificent fish dish on the way. Just wait till you taste it! It'll be heaven for a fish-lover like your good self."

Heaven?

"Excellent, I'm looking forward to it. I'm sure it won't disappoint." I look at Lydia.

"Okay, I'll leave you to enjoy cleansing your pallets for now."

"Thanks, Khushtar," Lydia smiles. Once his back is turned, she looks at me quizzically. "Are you okay, darling?"

I take the phone out of my pocket. "Yeah, I'm fine, honey. It's just that this has been kinda doing my head in. It bleeps every time I get a message on Facebook. Is there any way you can turn that off for me? And can you change the text alert tone as well? The sound of the one it's on at the moment cuts through me like a knife." *Or a meat cleaver.* "You know I'm not great with these things."

"Sure, gimme it here. I only had it on that tone because it was easy to hear and I didn't want to miss any messages from you, my lovely."

I smile and take a large mouthful of wine.

"All the bleeping will be notifications from 'The Lads' I take it?" she says, eyes down, pressing the screen.

"Yeah, probably."

"What have you lot been gossiping about lately?"

How come she hasn't mentioned it? Surely she knows.

"Just stuff about football . . . Max was starting to do my head in, though. You know what he's like sometimes, and Reggie and Joe were taking the bait. It was all becoming a bit tiresome, so that's why I want the bleepy alert thing turned off."

"There you go, that's it done." Lydia hands me back the phone. "Ah, here we are!"

"Two fresh sea bass with potato gratin and seasonal vegetables," Khushtar announces, proudly.

"Thank you, it smells lovely." Lydia rubs her hands together.

"Enjoy!"

"Thanks, Khushtar," I say.

I look down at the beady black eye staring up at me, so lifeless it could be plastic. But it smells divine.

"Couldn't the chef have done fillets?"

"Oh, don't worry, honey, I'll sort it for you." Lydia lifts my plate, places it next to hers and gets to work.

The soft flesh is placed neatly alongside the seasonal vegetables. I gawk at the ripped out spine and severed head. The plastic eye stares up, unforgiving, the mouth open from the shock of being stunned to death.

"Are you okay, honey? You're looking a bit green around the gills. Oh my God, you're sweating too. Darling, are you sure you're okay? What's wrong . . . Ryan?"

How come she hasn't mentioned it? Surely she knows. *Surely* she knows.

Dubya-Bush drinking oil from a crystal glass. The Joker, shoulder to shoulder, laughing at the sky. Plastic-eyed fish at Mr Willis's. *We're all full of dioxins*, they say in unison, mouths bleeding.

I place my hand on hers.

"I love you," I say.

I Love Your Heart

It's the way you embrace everything with such positivity. Every new person is a chance to make a new friend. And if you're rejected, you're never deflated. You just keep going, with spirit in your stride and a smile on your face. Everyone gets a chance no matter what they look like, where they're from, who they are.

You never read the papers.

Sadness is an opportunity to help, happiness an opportunity to share, and play, and run, and be. If you know how you came to be like this,

show me.

Run

From about 15 deep, I see a fat guy in an Arsenal top lining up in the front row. I glance at the runners either side of me to see if they've clocked him, but they're busy doing final stretches. I check the pocket in my shorts for the umpteenth time, making sure it's fully zipped and that the teeth aren't showing any signs of splitting apart.

Last fuckin' time, mate.
I'm done with this shit.
I'm turning my life around.
Getting fit, living clean and all that.

> *Ha ha ha ha ha ha*

I'm serious.
I've taken up running and I've been eating well.
Fed up feeling like shit and always
looking over my shoulder.

> *Ha ha ha ha ha, you're hilarious.*
> *Here's the gear and the address.*
> *Jimmy's expecting it midday on Sunday.*
> *There's a wee bit in there for you as well.*

I mean it, this is the last time.
After I leave here I'm getting a new phone.
I'll post the money through your door on Sunday
night, then you'll never see me again.

> *Ha ha ha ha ha ha*

There was no way I was missing my first 10k to deliver

shit for Hex. Luckily, the address he gave me is only a couple of miles north of the finish line. I look down at my new running shoes. Best purchase I ever made. Feels like I'm walking on a pair of massive sponges.

"What club are you with?" asks the guy next to me.

"Eh . . . I'm not in a club."

"You running for charity then? Or just for yourself?"

"Just for myself."

"Should maybe consider a club," he says, stretching his hamstring. "Helps keep you motivated. Good laugh as well."

"I've only been training about five weeks though," I say. "This is my first race."

"Really? Well, you look pretty fit to me. And anyway, clubs take people at all stages of their running career."

I stifle a laugh. I thought running was just running. Never thought career came into it unless you were someone like Mo Farah or Paula Radcliffe.

"If you fancy giving it a bash, come and see me at the finish line. Or if you can't find me, just look us up." He turns his back and points at the URL printed at the bottom of his vest.

"Okay, I might do that," I say, stretching my back.

"Zoinks! Look who's here!" He thumbs over his shoulder. I turn to see Scooby-Doo lining up towards the back. There's also a giant Smurf, cadets carrying massive backpacks and some bearded men dressed as panto dames.

"They must be roasting," I say, looking up at the sun working its way through the clouds.

"Totally. Last year I did a 5k for Children in Need dressed as Barney the feckin' dinosaur. Think I must've lost about a third of my body weight that day. The costume was soaking when I peeled it off."

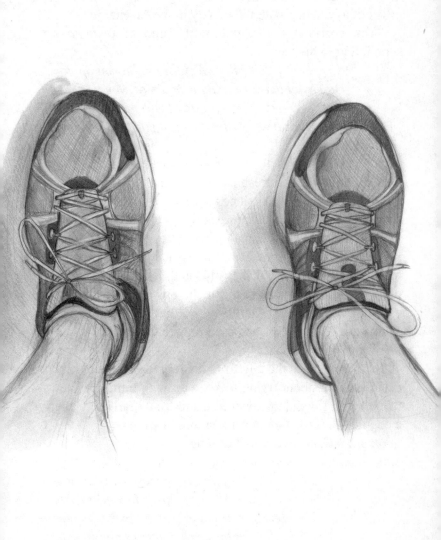

"Nice," I laugh.

When the gun sounds, everyone surges forwards. But on the left hand side bodies fall to the ground, the knock-on effect of a collision with the fat guy in the Arsenal top.

"You cost me a PB, you twat," one of them says, scrambling to his feet.

After the way we brought you up, too.
Don't you darken our door again till you're clean.
You hear me, Alexander?
Our name will not be brought into disrepute
on account of you.

About 2k in, I'm feeling good, knocking out a steady rhythm, enjoying the fresh air in my lungs and the sun on my face. It's been weeks since I used and ever since I started running, I've been picturing rocking up to Mum and Dad's looking like a normal human being, but with a medal round my neck and a bottle of Evian in my hand. She welcomes me in all smiles. Dad shakes my hand, tells me he's proud of me and that everyone has their slip ups, no big deal, want a cup of coffee, son? And I say yes, but no sugar, thanks. Mum says really? But you used to take three. And I say I know, but things change.

I can't even see the guy from the running club anymore. I had thought about trying to keep up with him, but knew that'd mean I'd end up knackered and would fall away after a couple of miles. Got to walk before I can run.

Look, it's the same gear as last time.
Same place, same supplier, same everything.

You're talking out your arse,
this is fuckin' inferior.
Tell Hex he better watch his fuckin' back
if he keeps giving us shit like this

and charging the fuckin' same.
That goes for you as well.

Halfway mark, but I'm starting to struggle. It feels like lots of folk have overtaken me and I'm starting to doubt myself. I can feel a little twinge in my right hamstring or it might be my mind playing tricks on me, like I'm looking for an excuse for slowing down. There's probably nothing wrong with my hamstring. Yes there is, that was a definite twinge! Was it fuck, Xander, you're slowing down because your junkie body is wondering what you're doing to it, just like an athlete's would if they suddenly started shooting up. That's crap, it can't be in shock, 'cos you ran 8k in the park last week. Yeah, but there was hardly anyone around, and no overtaking, plus this is 10k, that's two more, and there's a medal, and a t-shirt, and a banana.

Xander, I just can't do this anymore.
You've changed so much.
It's like I barely know you.

But, Tanya, no, wait.

At the next water stop, I grab two cups, drink one and throw the other over my head. My long-sleeved t-shirt gets a second soaking when a girl dodges a cup being thrown at her by her friend.

"Sorry about that," she laughs.

"No worries, I actually quite liked it." Her pal is red-faced but I can't tell if it's from embarrassment or exertion.

The water helps a little and I feel okay for the next kilometer or so. But then my legs begin to feel heavy, like cricket balls have been tied to my calves. More people overtake me as the water-fight girls shrink into the distance. I can still make out the dodger though, her blonde bun poking up over the heads of those around her.

Xander, man, if you help me deal,
you take a cut – cash _and_ gear.
You'll not need uni or any of that shite,
and you can get wasted whenever you like.

I start worrying about the money running out. I'll need to get a job, like normal folk. But what if you can't? What if employers question the gap in your employment history? You could go back to uni, pick up where you left off. Debt and a shite job, that's all uni gets you, Hex said. Then I remember Dad saying don't worry too much about the job market, son, things will pick up, and a good education is the most important thing anyone can possess, knowledge is power, power is success, and success is happiness, and you want to be happy, don't you, son? Yes, Dad.

I can still see the blonde bun, but it's drifting further and further away as the guilt of letting everyone down pulses through me. I think about pulling out, not wanting to add my race position to my growing list of disappointments. Everyone thinks you're a loser anyway, a degenerate junkie scumbag, a wart on the arse of society. There are people in the town that'll always associate you with skag. And all Tanya's pals hate you. So does Tanya. And the chances of bumping into Hex are high. Maybe you should just pull out and take that hit he gave you.

"Keep going, you're doing really well," shouts a random spectator, rapidly clapping his hands like a football captain geeing up his team. It's not directed at anyone in particular, just an enthusiast enjoying the event, admiring those who put themselves in for the race. There's a surge in pace and the fat guy in the Arsenal top pulls up alongside me. His face is nearly as red as his top, but he's not giving in, stubborn determination in his expression. He knows his body isn't built for speed – at least not at the moment – but he's finishing this race if it's the last thing he does. I feel bad for sniggering at him earlier, even though starting in the front row was a really stupid idea.

But he's no different to me. Trying to change; to prove something to himself; to leave the old him behind and race towards the new.

Tell you what, I'll shoot up with you.
You know I don't use any old shit,
so if this isn't right,
we'll go and sort Hex out together.
Deal?

Deal

Awwwwwwwwwww
$\qquad$ *w*
$\qquad$ *w*
$\qquad$ *w*
$\qquad$ *w*
$\qquad$ *w*

Yeah, but wait till it wears off

Your body's just
changing

As I pass the 9k sign into the last kilometer, I lock my eyes onto the blonde bun, which is now the size of a pea. Behind me I hear the random spectator encouraging the next wave of runners and the fat guy in the Arsenal top wheezing like a set of bellows that have been in an attic for 20 years. And I run

Run

Run

Run

Run

Run

Run away from
                    Run towards
          Run away from
                    Run towards
                              towards
                                   towards

Panting
     Sweating
     The bun gets closer.
Just put the knife down, Craigy.
Easy. Easy.
I'll sort this out.
You were right, good initial hit,
but something's not quite right about it.

                              Shit, fuckin' pigs!

Woa, woa, don't panic, just lay low!
Chances are they're not for us anyway.
Just put the knife away and pretend you're
talking to me, take your phone out,
show me a photo on it or something.
If we run like fuck carrying gear and a knife,
we're only going to attract attention.

Closer and closer. And I can now see her pal too. I think about Tanya, and Mum and Dad, and the texts on my phone. From junkies, from Hex, from Tanya telling me to stop texting her, from folk from uni wondering what happened, how come you just vanished off the face of the earth, how come you don't reply, how come you don't seem to give a fuck anymore, how come you're running away from growing up, from responsibility, what's your problem, the world too tough for you or something? And while I imagine the runners behind me are the devils of my past, snarling and foaming at the mouth, I know I'm running towards some of the same people, but with cap in hand, and I'm dreading it. But it has to be done.

When I reach the finish line, I slow to pick up my medal, t-shirt and some water, but I don't stop.

"Hey, well done, that's not a bad time for a first 10k," shouts the guy from the athletics club. I give him a thumbs up and keep running.

I head north over the park past children playing, couples out for walks, folk playing frisbee. A fox terrier runs alongside me so I try and outrun it, but it darts off to the call of its owner's whistle.

I decide that instead of giving Jimmy a freebie, I'll keep my bit and flush it when I get home. Might give my mobile a bath too and then go and buy a new one – new network, new number, new beginning. Then I'll maybe give Mum and Dad a phone, just to say hi.

I up my pace towards Jimmy's and I'm in such a groove, I could just run and run and run, until the spongy soles of my shoes wear through and the concrete rips my socks to shreds. And even if the skin on my feet was to grate to bursting and my flesh wore away till I was running on bone,
I don't think I'd stop.

Ella 21:18

Despite the crew doing their best to convince us everything's under control, I know it's only a matter of time before the second engine fails. It's noisy with toil, battling vicious winds as the cabin oscillates like a theme park ride. Oh my God, I'm going to die, I'm going to die, I'm going to die, I'm going to die. My mind's determined to convince me that my final moments should be spent analysing why my precious time *hasn't* been spent living life to the full, even though that isn't entirely the case. This can't be happening! Tell me this isn't happening! Somebody *has* to be taking the piss here. Fuck! The cabin drops like a kid letting go of a marble. I push back into my seat and grip the armrests, knuckles white. I look at the old woman in the window seat; straight as a board, facing forward, eyes closed. Come on T-Mobile you useless fucks! I need to speak to Shirley, I need to tell her I love her and that I'm sorry about Thursday, and to look after Holly. Oh my God, my little princess! Bottles, books and bags tumble down the aisle, clattering into ankles and seat fixings. Stomachs jump into mouths as the cabin drops again. The old woman reaches over the empty seat between us and squeezes my hand. `Listen to me son. This is the end, isn't it?` I nod, gulping. `I hate hearing all this screaming and swearing, it's upsetting me. You might` as fucking-well tell me now, Connor! You're seeing someone else, aren't you? You're shagging that little slut from the gym, aren't you? Aren't you? Have you had a good life? She squeezes my hand tighter. Yeah . . . yeah, I mean, there've been a few opportunities which I wish I had taken, which I didn't, but, you know, that's just . . . just . . . What about you? Have you had a good life? I've loved every minute of it. She smiles, and I can't help but smile back, warmed by the truth in her eyes. I'm Ella. Fuck! Fuck! Shit! Shit! Shit! Fuck! FUCK! Mark. It's a pleasure to meet you, Mark. Her nails dig into my hand and scrape short white lines into my flesh. I don't want to die in a panic. Just listen to everyone shouting and swearing and shrieking like banshees. That's no way to exit this wonderful world, now is it, Mark? Mummy, I'm scared! Why is everybody screaming and swearing? What's wrong with the aeroplane? Why can't the pilot fix it? I don't like it, Mummy! I don't like it! Make it stop! Make it stop, Mummy! Pleeeease! Pleeeeeeeeease! Well . . . eh . . . no. Good, I'm glad you agree. Ella pats my hand twice then grips it tight again. So how about you and I, we go out laughing. What do you say? Y . . . yeah . . . okay, why not? Great! Okay, listen, this is what we're going to do. Who did the safety checks on this plane? Eh? Surely there was a safety check done as standard? Take off your shirt. Eh? Take off your shirt and give it to me. I'll give you my dress and put a bit of make-up on you. Are you serious? I look into her eyes. She laughs at my expression. Well, we want to go out laughing, don't we? And you did say you were with me, didn't you? I'm sorry, sir, but I don't know who carried out the safety checks. Please try to remain calm. We're . . . We're doing everything we can to sort things out here. Well . . . y, yeah, but . . . But what, Mark? Oh, right, okay, come on then, let's get that dress off you, and by the way, how did you know that violet was my favourite colour? The joy in her expression shoots tingles up my spine. Intuition, she says, quickly tapping the side of her head. Yeah, well whoever they are, they're fucking inept! Okay, Ella, if you want my shirt, you're going to have to let go of my hand. After three. She looks forward. One . . . two . . . three. I undo the top few buttons of my shirt and whip it off like it's a jumper, and cringe at my hairy doughnut hanging over my seatbelt. For the love of God, will somebody pleeeease doooo something! I don't wanna die! I don't wannaaaaa dieeeeee! Okay, your turn, Ella. She takes a deep breath, lets go of her armrests and quickly pulls the bottom half of her dress up past her seatbelt. She steadies herself then pulls it over her head. I look at her wrinkly skin and withered, sagging breasts, badly supported by a deteriorating, discoloured bra. Right, give me that. She grabs my shirt, glowering at me for grimacing at her wilting body. I pull the flowery dress over my head, expecting it to smell of lavender or mothballs, but it doesn't. Laughter bursts through my lips at Ella drowning in my shirt. Looking good, Ella. Same to yourself, at least you will do once you've got that bottom half sorted. Sandra . . . Sandra, you do realise you mean the world to me, don't you? The absolute world. Mark, do you think you could tear that juice can and cut off my pony tail? I end up lacerating a finger but use the hair I manage to remove to make a bandage. Ella pulls out a lipstick from her bag and waits for the turbulence to get worse so it looks like it's been done by a three year old. Look, right, everyone just stay calm! If we all stay calm we can get through this together, right? Panicking isn't going to help anyone. Hysterical with laughter, Ella grips my hand so tight it's like she's trying to stop the blood flow. No! No! No! Fuuuck! Noooo! Tears freefall down her cheeks and drip off her chin onto my shirt. Her rapture's infectious, the vision of her joy distorted by my own tears as I crease up at her psycho haircut, a chunk of it matted with my blood, and I laugh harder at the prospect of a crazy against-all-odds survival. Why are you laughing? Eh? You think this is funny, you sick fuckers! At Ella and me turning up at the airport dressed like nutters, everyone looking at us while we're waiting for our bags. Don't call my friend a fucker; can't you see she's 109 years old? Oh, Mark, stop it, I'm going to have a heart attack! Here, put this in, dear, drown out that idiot. She passes me an earphone, which I stuff into my left ear. Keep looking at me, Mark, and keep laughing. And Mark? Yeah? Thank you. She presses play. We lock eyes and sing along to The Walker Brothers' *Make it Easy on Yourself.* When the second engine fails and the plane nosedives, Ella cranks the volume as high as it'll go. No! No! No! Fuck! Fuck! Fuck! Fuck! I glance at my watch. 21:18. And think of keys. I look back at Ella and laugh and laugh and laugh and laugh and laugh. Maaaaaake iiiit eeeeasyyy on yourseee-eelf. Maaaaaake iiiit eeeeeasyyy on yo

Sinkho

Some Tiffin

When you walk down the towpath, it's clear of the usual detritus. No broken bottles; no cans stuffed in the hedge; no shit smudged over the slabs. You let Rusty off the leash and he looks up, confused.

"Go on, then," you say, pointing down the path. He does a double-take then follows his nose to the hedge, tail wagging, floppy ears brushing the ground.

The park is clear. Not just of litter, but of people. You scan left and right, but there isn't a soul. You shield your eyes from the sun and look over to the old manor house. The clip end of Rusty's leash falls from your grasp and swings back and forth in silhouette, like a pendulum. You close your eyes for a few seconds, inhale the smell of freshly-cut grass and listen to the birds singing.

Rusty is bounding around, erratically changing direction, tongue hanging out. "Having fun there, pal?" You reach into your pocket for his ball. "What's this, Rusty?" He looks round and raises a paw in anticipation. You throw the ball as far as you can and he races towards it like his life depends on returning it to you.

"Good boy." He drops the ball at your feet, looks up and barks. You love how simple his happiness is. You throw it again and he runs, so fast it barely hits the ground before it's back in his mouth.

You walk towards the manor house and imagine living in it, working as a maid or a housekeeper, flirting with the owner, or perhaps a handsome butler. You picture elegant cars with white-wall tyres rolling up to the front of the house and the bourgeoisie being welcomed in to enjoy dinner parties and games of billiards. You'd be in charge of ensuring the guests' overcoats were suitably stowed in the cloakroom and that only the finest china was used to serve them tea and Victoria sponge.

Rusty in tow, you walk round the perimeter of the house, boots and paws crunching on gravel. It's as still as a photograph. You wonder if something happened during the night – that killed everyone, except a choice few. And you're one of them. And it's now your responsibility to find a mate and start the human race again! You could live in the manor house!

Laughing, you pick up Rusty's ball and throw it towards some rhododendrons. His enthusiasm leaves tracks in the gravel. You smooth them over with the sole of your boot as you walk towards the limestone steps that lead down to the rest of the park.

Rusty drops his ball at the foot of the steps, but you're distracted by the hum of a bumblebee pollinating a nearby daffodil. You move closer until you're only a few inches away. You think about taking a grainy photograph on your dated phone, but opt to enjoy the moment instead of trying to capture it. You watch it flit from flower to flower until the hum is nearly inaudible and its fluffy coat is lost on a palette of summer bloom. Rusty is waiting patiently for you to throw his ball.

"Go on, boy! Fetch!" You run after him, mimicking a panting dog. He increases speed and wins the race comfortably. Ball in mouth, he jumps up, tail wagging hard, grunting like a pig. You take his paws in your hands and dance him round in a circle.

"Let's go again!" You prise the ball from his mouth, throw it towards the bridge and shoot off as fast as you can. Rusty quickly pulls up level and then moves into the lead, his throaty glee so funny that you have to slow for laughing. But just before he reaches the ball, a golden labradoodle darts out from under the bridge and makes off with it.

"Jeffrey!" a shrill voice blares. "Put that down!"

Rusty doesn't know what to do and looks at you for answers. Jeffrey shakes his head and snorts, mouthing the ball as if he's trying to eat it. As you approach, a gaunt woman emerges from the shadows of the bridge.

"Leave, Jeffrey, leave!" She reaches into the pocket of her cagoule and lifts her hand in the air. Jeffery drops the ball instantly, darts over and is fed a treat. Rusty picks up his ball and quickly returns to your side. "Sorry about that," she smiles.

You worry that she clocked the terror in your expression, over which you had no control. Perhaps it was the way the light was shining that made her so alarmingly hideous.

"That's okay."

"He's just an excitable pup, aren't you, spud?" she says, ruffling Jeffrey's ears as he licks his lips. The sun shines on her crown and you notice matted clumps of thin hair where she's tried to apply cream. When she straightens, your eyes dart between her solitary front tooth – the focal point of her patchy yellow and black smile of irregular, cartoony teeth, like they've been drawn by a three-year-old at Halloween – and the deep, purple scar on her left cheek, which runs in a perfect arc from just below her temple to where her lips meet.

"How old is he?" you ask, looking at Jeffrey's fluffy face.

"Nearly 18 months. What about yours?"

"He's three." You reach down and pat his head.

"Aw, he's a cracker, isn't he? My sister used to have a springer spaniel." She crouches down. "What's his name?"

"Rusty."

"C'mere, Rusty!" she beckons, slapping her palms off her thighs. He's reluctant at first, but her friendly, upbeat voice draws him in and he pads over. "Aw, you're gorgeous, aren't you?" Jeffrey joins in, sniffing Rusty all over before licking the woman's face to remind her who's best. You stand awkwardly, looking down at the three-way embrace. Part of you wants to get involved but you decide against it. You want to tell the woman that Jeffrey's gorgeous too, but he's more daft-looking than anything else. He needs a haircut, his face like a big ball of wool. He looks up with a gormless expression, pink tongue hanging out the side of his mouth, as if questioning why you aren't joining in.

"Aw, you're a right cutie, aren't you?" He licks your wrist and gives you a look only dogs are capable of – *I'm your pal, love me, love me*. You tickle his belly and his eyes droop, as if you've taken out his batteries. Knees clicking, the woman stands up. The dogs start frolicking around, darting left and right, jumping on each other's backs, neither of them interested in the ball anymore.

As the woman watches them play, you notice a long, thin object covered in brown cloth protruding from her rucksack. You look around and the park is still empty.

"Okay, Rusty, come on then, pal."

"Before you head off," the woman says, reaching into the other pocket of her cagoule, "would you like some homemade tiffin?"

She presents it to you on her palm, neatly wrapped in cling film. You look at her misshapen, discoloured fingernails and picture her hands in the mixing bowl.

134

"No, thanks," you say, even though tiffin is one of your favourite treats.

"Really?" She looks disappointed. "It's my special recipe. Don't you like tray-bakes?"

"No, it's not that, I love them actually."

"So if it's not that, what is it?" She tilts her head slightly.

"Eh, it's just that I had a bar of chocolate earlier and I don't want to overdo it, you know. Trying to stay healthy and all that."

"Oh, come on, a little bit of tiffin isn't going to do you any harm, is it?" She pushes it closer. You look at her teeth and wonder if a lifetime of treats is responsible for their condition. She has kindness in her eyes, though, sitting bright and blue in an otherwise ill-favoured face.

"Well, okay then."

"Great! I've got a knife and some napkins in my bag, so we can have half each. None for you two," she says to the dogs. "This stuff is poison for four-legged friends I'm afraid."

She opens her bag, pulls out the long thin object and places it on the ground. A gust of wind blows over a corner of the cloth to reveal the jaws of a litter-picker. As she digs around in her rucksack, you do a quick scan. No litter. And still no people.

"Ah, here we are." She pulls out a plastic box containing napkins and a cheese knife. You look at her fingers as she peels the cling film off the tiffin, places it in the box and cuts it in half.

"Help yourself." She passes you a napkin.

"Thanks." You lift out the slightly smaller piece and place it on your napkin. The woman lifts the other to her mouth and takes a bite.

"Fire in," she says.

You take a small bite and feel the urge to cry.

"You've got real pieces of ginger in here, haven't you?"

"Oh, yes. This is *real* tiffin, made with ginger pieces and crushed ginger nuts. None of this Rich Tea nonsense. And the raisins are organic too."

"It's fabulous," you say, taking a bigger bite.

"I'm glad you like it . . . I'm Cara, by the way."

"Nancy." You extend your hand, which she shakes firmly, as if you're closing a business deal.

"Are you okay?"

"Yeah, sorry, it's just . . . your recipe . . . it's exactly how my grandma used to make it. We were really close . . . She passed away in the winter."

"Oh, I'm sorry. I didn't mean to upset you."

"No, honestly, it's fine. They're good memories. Every Christmas, she'd bake me a tray of either rocky road or tiffin. Tiffin like this. I tried to make it once, but it was nowhere near as good."

Jeffrey, now less interested in Rusty, looks up, mooching.

"No, Jeffrey! Go and play," Cara commands. Jeffrey trots off, looking over his shoulder, hoping she's joking.

"I can give you the recipe if you want."

"Really?"

"Sure. Me and Jeffrey will be here tomorrow about the same time. How about I write it down tonight and you can pick it up tomorrow?"

"That'd be great. Thanks."

"No problem. The secret is in the method and using good quality ingredients – and once you've got it, you've got it," she smiles. Her kind eyes smile too, diverting your attention from her hideous mouth and the little piece of tiffin stuck to the middle of her lone front tooth.

"Right, Jeffrey, come on, pal, home time." Jeffrey looks up from sniffing Rusty's bum and pads over. You're impressed at how obedient he is for a young labradoodle.

"Well, it was nice to meet you, Nancy."

"Yeah, likewise," you say. "Come on, Rusty! Time to go. Bring your ball!"

Rusty picks up his ball and trots over, snout in the air.

"Good boy!" You bend down to ruffle his ears. "Same place, just here under the bridge?" But when you look up, Cara and Jeffrey are gone.

You lick the tiffin crumbs from your napkin, fold it and put it in your pocket. You pick up Rusty's ball and throw it back towards the grounds of the manor house – and your dreams.

You see no-one on your way home. When you arrive, you desperately need the toilet. You flick the light switch and the extractor fan whirs into action. You close the door, sit down and pee, relief tingling through your body.

The bulb pops and the whir cuts.

A whimper escapes. You sit in darkness, listening to your now amplified stream, and slap your tongue against the roof of your mouth to make that flavour last as long as possible.

Hot Cakes

I think you've done a brilliant job, darling.

Really?

Yes! I'm so impressed with all the work you and Flick have done. I can't wait for next weekend.

But do you think people will buy tickets?

Absolutely! I think they'll sell like hot cakes.

But why would anyone want to buy a hot cake? Wouldn't they burn their mouth? I've never had a hot cake before.

It's just an expression, sweetheart. And you have had a hot cake before. What about Gran's Eve's Pudding?

That's not a cake, it's a pudding. It's even got the word pudding in its name. A Victoria Sponge is a cake, but who would want a hot one of them? The jam would be like lava from a volcano. You'd have to wait for it to cool down. Then it wouldn't be a hot cake.

Kelly, when someone says 'they'll sell like hot cakes', they just mean–

And my favourite cake that Gran makes is refrigerator cake. That's the opposite of a hot cake!

Kelly, honestly, darling, you're overrea–

Even the supermarkets don't sell hot cakes. They sell hot chicken and hot pies and hot sausage rolls, but not hot cakes. No-one wants hot cakes, Mum! If they did, the supermarkets would have them. Flick! Flick! No-one's coming to our show!

Secret Weapons

Friday the 2ⁿᵈ, 11.04am.

As I enter the lecture theatre, I see McDonald's cups and confectionery wrappers strewn amongst rucksacks and fidgeting feet under benches awash with blobs of disposed chewing gum, some of which will have fresh bubbles of saliva dying upon them. After the lecture, these become *my* responsibility, as apparently it's not in the janitorial staff's job description – and if I leave the place like a dump, other lecturers will complain. Sure, I could tell them not to do it, but it just lands on deaf ears; some even laugh at the suggestion, like they have the authority to do what they want just because their fees have been paid.

Mobile phones sit in front of nearly every student like name plaques and beep, ring and vibrate as I'm setting up the PC and sorting out the slides. Only a handful appear to be doing the reading and a group of guys in the middle of the back row have huddled together to watch a video on someone's iPhone. I take a deep breath.

"Right, come on, settle down everybody, we've got plenty to get through today so let's get the notes and the textbooks out and make a start . . . Guys, guys, come on, simmer down, it's time to begin," I say to the group who've just erupted in laughter at whatever was on the iPhone. "And what's with the McDonald's, Trevor? It's not lunch time for another hour and a half yet."

"Eh, I think you mean an hour and 26 minutes," Trevor says, looking at his watch. "You're four minutes late. And this is obviously my breakfast, not my lunch."

"Yes, well if nothing else, at least you're observant, Trevor. Now come on, ditch the burger and the milkshake and get the books out."

"It's Diet Coke actually," he sneers.

"Well, whatever it is, will you please just finish it off or get rid of it, okay?"

"Are you on a diet, like, Trevor?" asks Emma, leaning across from a few seats away.

"No, I'm not, Emma," Trevor says, standing up. "I just want to maintain my perfection." He runs his hands down his torso like he's in a boy band music video.

"That's enough! Sit down, Trevor! . . . Now, who's done the reading on schemas?"

"Has that got anything to do with housing schemes or that?" Emma asks.

"Yeah, like where your family's from, Emma? Mind that telly programme *Benefits Street?* That's you and your family that is."

Laughter ripples through the class.

"Shut your face, Trevor! Like you're from Beverley Hills, eh? You cheeky dick."

"Right, that's enough, and mind your language, Emma," I say. "Now, has *anyone* done the reading on schemas?" I scan the whole class. The mature students in the first couple of rows nod their heads. "Okay, anyone from the third row back?"

Silence.

"Okay, well, while I'm setting up the PC and sorting out the slides, will you all please have a skim read of pages 46-48 in your textbooks on schemas? And for those of you who have read it already, well, it won't do you any harm to jog your memory. After all, there just might be an exam question on this material," I wag a finger. "Hint hint."

Trevor drops his McDonald's cup to the floor, the ice rattling on impact, like it's a signal to start chatting. Once I've set up the PC and my slide show is ready to run, I perch on the edge of my desk and wait for them to pick up on my non-verbal cue. But they don't, of course. The guys in the middle of the back row have huddled together again to watch another video. I'm looking directly at them, but it's like they haven't even acknowledged my arrival, let alone listened to what I said about skimming those pages. Maybe they think because there are 70-odd folk in the class they somehow become invisible; lost in the crowd.

The mature students in the first couple of rows wear expressions I've become all too used to. I bet they weren't expecting this carry on when they took the plunge and signed up for a diploma. God, I feel sorry for them, especially those who have paid their own fees *and* are paying for childcare because their other halves need to work to pay the bills. Thing is, they really want to learn too. They're keen and enthusiastic and want to go on to university to study for a degree. But here they are, sharing their 'learning experience' with this lot, who're only here because they can't get a job, can't be bothered getting a job, or because they had to do *something* after school and decided to just do what their pals were doing. At least it'll buy them another couple of years before they have to make a *proper* decision.

I glance over to Grace, Johnny's note taker. Johnny is on the autistic spectrum and is patiently awaiting his opportunity to learn. Grace's expression communicates a message of good luck, a timely reminder of how pissed off she is at having to put up with this nonsense week in, week out. We exchange a nod. I stand up and clap my hands.

"Okay, folks, now, can anyone give me a definition of a schema?"

"No, nobody cares," Trevor shouts.

"Is that right, Trevor? And tell me, how can you make that judgement when you don't even know the definition yourself, eh?"

"He's got a point there, Trevor," Emma squeaks. "How can you make that judgement, eh?"

"Shut it, you. Who asked you anyway?" he retorts.

"Well, I did, Trevor," I say. "The question was directed at anyone willing to answer it."

"See! So don't tell me to shut it, I'll chip in if I want, alright?"

"Well, come on then, smartarse, what is a schemie then?"

"A schemA, Trevor," I say, "not a schemIE, a schemA."

Trevor ruffles his stupid hair and leans forward. "Like it matters anyway. All this social psychology stuff is nothing but a lot of crap. I mean, seriously, how is knowing this drivel going to help me get a job, eh?"

One of the mature students turns round. "Will you please stop being a nuisance? Some of us are here to learn."

"Oooooh, some of us are here to learn," Trevor mocks. "I'll tell you what, right – if anyone in this room gets a job talking to folk about schemies, I'll run down the high street naked."

"I've already got that job, Trevor. In fact, I'm doing it right now," I say, grinning inside.

"Feel bumped, Trevor," Emma celebrates, clapping her hands. "Looks like you'll be stripping off then, eh? I think you should do it right here, right now, in front of everyone. That'll teach you for being all mouth. Come on then, whip them off . . . I'd quite like to see what's under there actually."

144

"Oh, is that right, baby? Well maybe me and you could have a little chat after class, so I can . . . let you down gently." Trevor's clearly unfazed by my attempt to embarrass him.

"Cheeky bastard!" Emma says. "I am prime stuff I'll have you know."

People laugh, but none louder than Donna, who's looking at her phone.

I raise my voice. "Right, that is enough! Can we please get back to the task in hand here? So, come on, what about you, Emma, I noticed you at least glanced at the textbook. Can you give us a definition of a schema?"

Donna bursts out laughing.

"Eh, going to stop laughing while I'm trying to answer a question!"

"What's so funny, Donna?" I say.

"Eh, nothing," she says through her giggles.

"And do you usually laugh at nothing, Donna?"

"Eh . . . eh . . . eh, sometimes."

"I don't think so. So, come on, what's the joke? If it's so funny, I'm sure the whole class would like to hear it."

I can't believe I just said that. *If it's so funny, I'm sure the whole class would like to hear it.* I swore I'd never use clichés like that, but it just slipped out, thanks to this lot.

"Yeah, come on then, Donna, let's hear what's so funny," Emma castigates.

"Alright then," Donna says.

Bloody hell.

"What was the last thing Hitler said to his men before they got in their tanks?"

"What?" one of the mature students says, rolling her eyes, not even bothering to turn round.

"Get in your tanks, men," Donna blurts out in a high-pitched giggle, which goes on and on and on. A handful of folk titter. Some shake their heads and sigh. Others just look confused.

"My sides are splitting, Donna . . . Right, can we *please* get back to the task in hand! Emma – definition of a schema – in your own time.

"Okay, so, see if I was to, like . . . eh . . . so if, like . . . if I was to, like . . . think about a doctor, right, I'd think about someone who, like, knows stuff about medicines and that, but has got really bad handwriting. And I would, like, think that because . . . because my head tells me that that's what I should think about when I think about a doctor. Is that . . . right?"

"Well," I say, scratching my neck, "you're along the right lines there, Emma. You just need to think more about–"

"Yeah, well done, Emma," Trevor interrupts. "Happy days, double thumbs, that's you just signed up for 50 grand a year."

See if I have issues with other classes, all I have to do is remind them that they're adults; that this is Higher Education and if they're not interested, well, they know where the door is. That tends to do the trick. In certain circumstances, if a class has been particularly unruly, I've had to print off ground rules and talk through them, or remind the students of them before I begin teaching:

Turn mobile phones off before lectures
Do not talk while I or others are talking
In group tasks, everyone must contribute
Speak out if you are being distracted by others
Leave the lecture theatre/classroom as you found it

And again, such action tends to be effective. But I don't like enforcing rules on a new class at the beginning of term as I feel it puts them on the back foot. I make the judgement over time as to when it is necessary to introduce them, if it is, indeed, necessary at all. And if I do, yeah, sometimes attendance drops but, as far as I'm concerned, the students who are keen to learn are at least given that opportunity without any distraction. Plus it makes my life a lot easier. So it's not like I'm soft or a walkover, or easy to ignore or take the piss out of, it's just that I've been given this bloody . . . class.

The mature students and Grace have made a handful of polite complaints, which is now cause for concern as things clearly haven't improved. This lot make up their own rules as they go along and despite going from politely asking them to quieten down to calmly encouraging them to leave, to issuing ground rules, to threatening to leave myself, all are met with giggles, faces of 'yeah right, who do you think you are?' or heads down, asleep on books.

And then there's Trevor, who has hair like he's been caught in a wind tunnel, much to the admiration of most of the young girls in the class. He's obnoxious, loud, rude and narcissistic, the kind of boy that attracts many a young innocent because he's 'adventurous' and 'dangerous', and because they suddenly have the liberty to explore, free from the shackles of any interfering parents.

"I've got a schemie for teachers," Trevor says. "Someone that just stands in front of a group of people and tells them things they'll never need to know ever again in their entire lives, ever."

"So why are you on the course then, Trevor? You're not a prisoner here. You're here allegedly because you want to be. So come on, tell everyone. Why are you on the course?"

"Something to do, isn't it? Better than being on the dole."

During the ten minute job of tidying up after the lecture, I see Grace standing by the exit. I've no idea how long she's been there and wonder if she heard me cursing when I came across discarded Maltesers trodden into the carpet, the explosion of malty crumbs difficult to prise from the fibres, especially when merged with half melted chocolate skidmarks.

"Can I speak to you for a moment?" she asks.

"Sure," I reply, "as long as you don't mind me continuing to tidy while we speak – this is already munching into my lunch break."

"No problem," she says, "I'll give you a hand."

Grace tells me of a contact she has, a man in his 50s who has a lot of experience in dealing with unruly and disrespectful classes. She says that he'd be willing to meet in town one night to discuss some techniques; share his wisdom; give me some sort of plan of attack.

"Here's his telephone number." She hands me his business card.

Alex Ricketts PhD, PG Dip, BA (Hons)

"Thanks," I say. "I'll give him a ring later on."

"I know a lot of people in Higher Education," Grace says, "and I know you're not a bad teacher."

"Thanks, Grace. I appreciate you saying that."

"And if I'm honest, I don't know many who would be able to handle that lot. I've never seen anything quite like it before."

"Neither have I. I'm seriously hoping it's a one-off."

Grace looks sympathetically at my exhausted face. I smile, grateful for her intervention – and because it's seven whole days before I need to endure the class from hell again.

In the staff room, I get chatting to Roland, a jolly, upbeat character who's been teaching for over 20 years. He points at my tired eyes though, asking if I was out drinking last night. Embarrassed, I think up an excuse about a barking dog keeping me awake. Then I think about Crystal, my ex. We had talked about getting a dog as a prelude to starting a family. That's until she decided, the week after I was given a permanent contract, to reveal that she wanted to travel the world while she was still young.

"How are you getting on with your groups this trimester?" Roland asks, just as I'm about to take my coffee back to my desk.

"Fine," I say. "They're all fine."

Back in my office, I flop onto my chair, sip my coffee and send a text to Alex Ricketts, enquiring when he'd be free for a chat. He replies immediately:

Monday. 6.15pm. Hathaway House Hotel. And bring your CV.

When I get home, I fall asleep on the couch and wake up hours later to the sound of my phone. It's my mum asking how my day's been. She phones more regularly now that Crystal's gone. I tell her everything's fine but just really busy, hence the tired voice. She reminds me that being busy is better than being bored and that I should be really proud that I've got a permanent post in this day and age, and that I did the right thing not going with Crystal, and that there'll be other girls, and that I should come round for my dinner more often, and that Dad could do with a hand putting up a cabinet in the bathroom, and blah and blah and blah. I say 'uh-huh' lots.

Monday the 5th, 6.14pm.

The hotel lounge is cosy, a coal fire ablaze behind the mandatory protective guard. In one corner sits a couple on a green leather sofa, their knees touching and eyes locked. In another, on a burgundy Chesterfield, is a well-dressed man in his 50s, legs crossed, reading glasses on, flicking through the pages of *The Guardian*. His black trousers ride up his shins, drawing attention to his navy blue socks and well-polished black brogues. As I approach, he dips his newspaper and peers at me over his glasses.

"Alex Ricketts?"

"It's Doctor Ricketts," he replies. "Have a seat, nice to meet you."

"Oh, my apologies, Doctor. Nice to . . . meet you too."

As I sit on the Chesterfield opposite, he folds his newspaper, leans forward and extends his hand, which I tilt and then shake firmly, maintaining eye contact throughout.

"So, I believe you have a shower of wasters that are causing you hassle?" he asks, getting straight to the point.

"Yes, Doctor, they certainly are a problematic bunch."

"Call me Alex," he says. "It was a test – to see if you would adhere to the rule I had imposed on you from the off. Tell me, do you use ground rules with your classes?"

"Eh . . . some of them. It depends on–"

"*Some* isn't good enough. It has to be all or nothing. For the classes you *do* use them for, do you introduce them on day one?"

"No, not always, I–"

"That's problem number two then." He leans forward in his seat and removes his glasses. "Now, let's pretend you and I have been talking for about an hour and all along you've been calling me Alex – and then suddenly, completely out of the blue, I insist that you call me Doctor Ricketts. How would you feel?"

"Well, probably a bit confused."

"Correct! So you get the message then?"

I nod.

"Good. Now, do you fancy a drink?"

"Eh . . . yeah, a drink would be good."

"Okay, walk with me." He stands and claps his hands together once, as if he's giving a dog a command. "Just leave your things where they are, they'll be perfectly safe, people know me round here."

"Oh, okay," I say, tucking my briefcase into the side of the Chesterfield – but as I stand erect, Alex puts his arm around me and, squeezing my shoulder, he presses my body to his, invading my personal bubble. I glance over to the couple on the sofa but they're so caught up in each other, they don't notice what's going on. Alex is looking at me with expectation so I slowly mirror his embrace and as soon as my hand touches his outside shoulder, he leans in to speak in my ear.

"If some little prick is constantly taking the piss, take him out the class for a quick word, but make sure you've got good reason to do so, like something to do with his student loan. If your reason's not believable, he's not going to budge. Your timing is paramount. About half an hour into the class is ideal. Try and tie it in so that what you're talking about to everyone acts as a reminder that you need to speak to him in person – there and then – about an important matter. If your reason involves money, he'll capitulate, no doubt about it. Then, when you get him outside the lecture theatre, look all around you, making sure no-one's nearby. Then look straight at him.

Alex drops his arm and turns. He's looking directly into my eyes. In fact he's looking *through* my eyes, as if he's trying to read my thoughts or see my soul. I hold his gaze but going from no eye contact to this type of eye contact is really quite unsettling. He slowly moves his face towards mine until the tips of our noses are nearly touching.

"And say *Get yourself to fuck.*"

He maintains his gaze for a few more seconds . . . and then breaks. The couple in the corner are sharing a gooey-eyed wordless moment of love, so the room is silent and still. And then, just as I'm about to say something, he puts his arm round me again, which I find myself automatically mirroring, as if we're playing *Simon Says*.

"When you re-enter the lecture theatre, make sure you slam the door, and I mean slam it like you've never slammed a door before. If the little prick has a bag or other bits and bobs, get someone to collect them together and bring them down to you – that's *get*, not ask, *get*. Then just open the door and throw them on the floor without looking at him. This'll reinforce how serious you are and it buys you an optional second door slam."

"Okay . . . I'll definitely try that," I say, feeling excitement in my bones at the look it could generate on Trevor's face.

"Good. Right, whisky!" Alex drops his arm and points towards the bar at the opposite side of the foyer.

"You know, Alex, I didn't actually introduce myself earlier, I must apologise for . . . "

"Don't worry, I know who you are, Grace has filled me in. Now, come on, let's get that drink." He struts off across

the foyer into the bar at the opposite side, his gait and posture confident, but not arrogant.

"Two 12-year-old malts please, no ice, just a splash of water," Alex says to the bartender, taking out his wallet. "Tell me," he says, now addressing me. "Would you say you're a strong person?"

"Eh . . . I don't think anyone's ever asked me that before." His expression and silent response tells me that that's not an answer. "I'd say I'm *fairly* strong."

He reaches over and squeezes my bicep. "Yes, I'd agree, but what about strength of character? Yes or no?"

"Eh . . . I don't think it's as cut and dried as that to be honest."

"Yes or no?"

"I can't answer such a question with yes or no," I try to reason. "I mean . . . I'd say I'm strong in some respects, but–"

"But what?"

"But . . . need to improve in others."

"That's the correct answer," he says, handing me a glass and chinking them together in celebration. I sip the whisky, which is delicious, and feel the alcohol give my brain a warm, fuzzy hug. "You're strong because you tilted my hand when you shook it. I offered you my hand with my palm facing down slightly to indicate that I'm in charge, but you tilted it to make things equal between us, highlighting that no-one should have the upper hand before anything has been discussed. And you did this despite me playing the Doctor Ricketts trick on you, so well done."

"Eh . . . thanks," I say.

"But what about me putting my arm round you? Didn't you feel uncomfortable, given that you'd only met me a few minutes beforehand?"

"Well . . . yeah, if I'm honest, I did find it a bit . . . weird."

"Okay, so first of all, thank you for being honest, it's a good quality in a person. But more importantly, why didn't you take control of the situation if it was making you feel uncomfortable?"

"Well, I suppose I didn't want to offend you by appearing unfriendly or . . . eh, unaccommodating."

"Take more control. You could've addressed the situation without coming across as unfriendly, couldn't you?"

I sip my whisky. "I suppose."

"Okay, so here's what I want you to do. When you get home tonight, replay the situation in your head and then send me an email detailing how you would deal with it if you could live it over. Okay?"

I take another sip. "Okay. But didn't you do it as a means of emphasising your mechanism for dealing with Trev, eh, a troublesome student?"

"Partly, yes, but does that mean you think that I couldn't have communicated said mechanism without putting my arm around you?"

" . . . "

" . . . "

"No, I suppose not."

Alex downs his whisky in one big, satisfying gulp, places his empty glass on the bar and asks the bartender for another. "Same again? Or would you like something different?"

I down what I have left and manage, I think, to hide my urge to cough. "Same again sounds good. If I didn't like 12-year-old malt whisky, I'd have said earlier, and please, let me pay for this one."

He smiles, and saying nothing, turns on his heels and walks away, presumably back to the lounge. Once I have the whiskies, I make my way through to find him back where he was, face buried once again in his newspaper. I get a strong sense of déjà vu, the glasses in my hands and the absence of the couple in the corner the only obvious differences.

"Ah, thank you," he says, taking the glass and instantly lifting it to his lips. "Now tell me more about this class."

"Ffffff, where do I start? It's the worst class I've ever had. They just don't seem to care whatsoever. How much has Grace told you?"

"Quite a lot," he replies, "but I just want to make sure that what you say and what she has told me matches up. It's not that I don't trust her, I'm just someone who likes confirmation."

We chat for a while about the class. He nods as I give him examples of some of the behaviour I've had to endure, which echoes a lot of what Grace has already told him.

"Okay," he says loudly, punctuating the end of my list of examples. "So, in future, regardless of which class it is or which level you're teaching at, set your ground rules on day one, and be stronger in character. For this crowd you're having trouble with at the moment, try out what we spoke about on the class joker and see what kind of response you get. But, if I'm entirely honest, based on the information I have from both you and Grace, it looks like you're going to need some secret weapons."

"Secret weapons?"

"Yes, secret weapons. Now, did you bring your CV as I asked?"

"I did," I say, reaching for my briefcase.

But it's gone!

I leap from my chair and search for it, erratically slapping the leather where it should be as if trying to summon it back.

156

"Shit! I've got important documents in that briefcase. My memory sticks, my CV, this year's exam questions! Tell me this isn't happening!"

I dash over to the green sofa where the loving couple was.

"Those bastards must've nicked it!" I check all around and under the sofa, which I realise makes no sense. I mean, why would anyone nick something and then just leave it behind?

"You looking for this?" Alex says, cool as the proverbial cucumber, the case lying on his lap.

"Oh, thank God!" I say, the relief tingling up my spine. "Wait a . . . hang on a minute, did you have it the whole–?"

"Too trusting!" Alex barks.

"Excuse me?"

"I said you're too trusting! You'd only known me for, what, two minutes, and you trusted me when it came to a case that contains important documents? Are you mad?"

"Well, no, but Grace–"

"Don't you know about Grace's criminal record?"

"WHAT?"

"Gotcha!" he says, head tilted, finger in the air. "However, I know for a fact that you don't know Grace well enough to know whether or not she has a tendency to steal, or arrange others to steal on her behalf." He rests the briefcase on the floor and stands up. "You're too trusting. And while I'm flattered that you *did* trust me, you have to learn to speak up. There were two other people in the room for heaven's sake! The fact that they were engrossed in each other to the extent that they probably didn't even notice us is just pure luck. Don't just accept what people tell you! Think about it! Challenge it! Check it! Show you're in control! If a class like your class from hell gets even a sniff of a lack of control, they'll capitalise on it." He steps forward, his expression softening. "And who ends up suffering? You. Who ends up stressed? You. Who ends up sleep deprived? You. And the kick in the arse is that, deep down, all you want to do is inspire them," – he lightly prods me in the solar plexus – "give them some direction, help them become better people, rounded learners, critical thinkers, good communicators, competent problem solvers blah blah blah blah blah. Am I right?"

I don't know whether I want to smack him in the face or hug him tight and weep on his shoulder. "Yeah . . . you are right."

He puts a hand on my shoulder. "I'm not saying you shouldn't be trusting, far from it. I just used it as an example of you not exercising enough control. When you're with that class, do you feel in control?"

"No. No, I don't."

He removes his hand. "Then you're going to need some secret weapons."

We sit down. I pick up my briefcase and stroke it like it's a sleeping dog, tingles of relief rippling through me.

"Now, can I have a quick look at your CV please?" Alex says, returning to his whisky.

"Of course." I click open the latches.

Alex seems impressed with my CV and we have a lengthy discussion, which allows me to reflect on how I go about my day-to-day work.

Then he gives me some secret weapons. And a shield.

A couple of hours later my head is buzzing, the combination of the Alex Ricketts experience and several 12-year-old malts. Alex opts for one more whilst waiting for his taxi, carefree about it being a weeknight, while I hope the walk home will help clear my head and give me a ticket for a good night's sleep.

I present a straight hand. "Thanks very much for tonight, Alex, it's very much appreciated."

Alex stands, smiling, and shakes my hand firmly. "It's Doctor Ricketts to you."

Friday the 9th, 11.28am

S L A M !

The force behind the slam cracks the wood of the doorframe, but thankfully the long, thin window in the centre of the door remains intact, through which I can continue my enjoyment of Trevor's reaction. As the class goes ohhhhhhhhhhhhhhhhhh, we lock eyes, revulsion in mine, bewilderment in his. I consider for a second that I could've taken things too far. Telling a student to get themselves to fuck is one thing. Telling them you're going to pan their cunt in is another. But I'm buzzing on it. I keep staring until *he* breaks the deadlock, dipping his head to digest my words.

"Frankie, bring Trevor's things down here. Now!"

Face twisted, Frankie tosses Trevor's phone and notebook into his bag and brings it down.

"That's all, back to your seat," I say, dismissing him with a hand.

I open the door. Trevor is leaning against the wall, but straightens as I approach him. I hold out his bag, but as he reaches to receive it, I let go and it thuds to the floor. His lips toy with a smirk, but it comes to nothing when he raises his head to see me looking through him, Ricketts-style.

"Beat it. And don't come back until you're ready to act like an adult."

With no response, he picks up his bag and scuffs his way down the corridor, jeans hanging off his arse. I watch him until he's gone. When I walk back into the lecture theatre, it's thick with the sound of chatter.

S L A M !

The crack deepens.   The class falls silent.

Grace and some of the mature students are smiling, delighted that I've successfully ejected the class clown. Johnny is the only one who looks no different, as if all along he was expecting something like this to happen. I don't feel like me. I feel like an intruder. It feels good. So instead of walking back to behind my desk, which I use as a shield, I walk to the middle of the front row and stand tall.

But I feel exposed and vulnerable and can feel my legs shaking, so I start pacing about, presenting it as confidence when really it's so no-one clocks my trousers waving about like ferns in a breeze.

"So, as I was saying – before we were rudely interrupted – there are three types of attribution, namely stable, internal and global." My voice is louder and clearer than it's ever been before, but it's all too much too soon for the class, whose way of dealing with my sudden execution of authority . . . is to laugh at it, or look at each other with gaping maws as if sharing a cruel twist in a soap. I do my best to battle on undeterred, but I can feel defeat slowly consuming me as I sink into the quicksand of my new exposed position, my control drifting as the minutes expire.

I can see the half-moon of Donna's baseball cap, her head thrown back in raptures at a joke on her phone. Sleepy-eyed Jenna has her head on her notebook, the job of staying awake all too much for her. Dave and Gareth are taking turns to twist each other's nipples, Emma is eating a cupcake and Alistair has let off, his peers laughing, pulling their jumpers up over their noses or wafting away his toxic anal gasses with notebooks. A biro strikes one of the mature students on the neck, an ill-judged throw by one of Alistair's cronies in retort to his noxious release. Grace looks over with sorrowful eyes, her smile, and the smiles of the mature students, gone. Thank God it's over for today.

When I get to the staff room, Roland, jolly as ever, tells me that external auditors are coming in in a fortnight to evaluate 'standards of teaching' and that an auditor can come into any class at any time. He also tells me that I look stressed and tired, which is the best thing anyone can say to someone who's stressed and tired.

Friday the 16th, 10.56am.

I perch on the desk and eyeball them as they arrive. On the screen behind me, in large black capital letters, are the ground rules. I glance at Trevor, who's sitting quietly, leafing through his notebook. Once everyone's in, chatting, shouting, eating, swearing, I take a wooden ruler from my drawer and rap it off my desk so hard it stings my fingers.

"Right! Before we start, can I please remind you of the

ground rules we spoke about earlier in the year. Rule number one – Turn mobile phones off before lectures. Everyone do this . . . NOW."

Revulsion echoes throughout the room as phones are lifted, turned off and then thrown back down in a domino rally of thuds. I cover the remaining rules, placing equal importance on each as they continue to talk over me. Donna is making it blatantly clear that her phone is still on as she's fiddling with buttons and chortling away to herself. I'd love to throw a

perfectly timed 5p coin at her gaping gob as she guffaws towards the ceiling. I imagine how her expression would change when the silver strikes her tonsils and she retches panicked and flummoxed, seeking sympathy from her neighbour. That'd teach her to laugh all the way through my attempts at trying to inspire her, trying to make her worth something, trying to make her more employable.

"Okay, now that you've been reminded of the ground rules, which I *highly* recommend you stick to, we can begin today's lecture, which is on Freud's theory of psychosexual development. We'll be zooming in on the first three stages, namely the oral, anal and phallic."

"Hey, Emma, you like a bit of anal, don't you?" Gareth shouts.

Raging, Emma spins in her seat "What did you just say, Gareth? That's totally out of order! What right have you got to say that to me, eh? You prick. You're the one who puts the psycho in psychosexual."

Before Gareth can retort, sleepy-eyed Jenna's phone rings. I race up the stairs and grab it. "I'm confiscating this until the end of class, Jenna. You can collect it then."

I notice a couple of shocked faces in the crowd, although

Jenna seems completely unfazed, her top lip curled in indifference. I put her phone in the top drawer of my desk, lock it and continue with my lecture as if nothing had happened. A few minutes later, Frankie's phone rings. Once I've wrestled it off him, I march back to my desk, but instead of putting it in the drawer, I rest it on top. I open the middle drawer, lift out a mallet and look up at Frankie. When I raise it above his precious phone, his jaw drops and the colour drains from his face.

"Don't tempt me," I say. "You don't want to push me . . . Isn't that right, Trevor?"

Trevor pretends to write notes to minimise the awkwardness. People around him snigger. Some of the mature students look horrified, others just fed up. Johnny rests his head in his hands, disheartened and discouraged, his opportunity to learn blighted by the idiots behind him. I return the mallet and close the drawer.

"Can I assume that you know I'm not joking about the ground rules now then? Things have got to change here. Now if you don't mind, there are people in this room who want to learn, so let's bash on with today's lecture without any further distraction, okay?"

I'm pleased to have got through most of the lecture without too much of a disturbance. The mature students are giving me the impression they're enjoying the juicy topic and many of them have taken several notes. Even some of the others, with the absence of their gadgets, seem to be paying more attention and have taken down a few points here and there. But, with about 15 minutes to go, unrest is again beginning to bubble. Bellies are rumbling and people are becoming fidgety and irritable as lunch time looms. Alistair is playing drums with his fingers, Emma is nattering in her neighbour's ear and little pockets of laughter blister here and there, although they're stifled, most of the time, when I cast admonishing stares. It looks like Dave and Gareth are trying to give each other discreet dead legs and Frankie and his mates are chatting away like they're in a cafe.

"Eh, you lot up there. Yes, you, you, you and you. Have you already forgotten the ground rules?"

"You what?" Frankie says.

"You heard me. Abide by the rules or get out!"

"Fucking make me."

A phone rings. Jessica, who sits a few seats along from Frankie, stands up and begins to prise her phone from her jeans' pocket. I run up the stairs.

"Give me that," I growl, lunging at it. "And what did you say, Frankie?"

"That's assault!" Jessica cries. "My uncle's a cop and I'm going to get you done for assault!"

"You heard me fine, I said FUCKING MAKE ME!" Frankie stands and puffs out his chest.

"You're not getting away with this," Jessica screeches. "I'll get you done for theft and indecent behavior."

"Come on then, I'm waiting to be chucked out your class here. What you going to do, eh? You fucking bully!"

The threats and insults come thick and fast as I walk backwards down the stairs, almost falling over at one point. A few of Frankie's mates have joined in, Trevor included. Pens and notebooks are thrown at me as Jessica continues to screech and point. Other girls begin backing her up and the angry noise builds and swells, a monster growing heads by the second, seeking justice, retribution, blood. I open the middle drawer.

With every shot, I step closer to Frankie until all four cartridges are discharged. Screams ring out as everyone ducks for cover. Grace, clutching her chest, tries to stand, but her legs buckle beneath her and she falls to the floor with a thud.

"Oh my God! Someone call an ambulance! Grace has had a heart attack!"

10.47pm

I sip my special tea and reminisce about the looks on their faces, especially after I pointed the finger of blame at them. Grace's performance was brilliant. She could really make it as an actor. The replica revolver, which I borrowed from the local theatre, sits on my coffee table next to some dirty mugs and unread Sunday paper supplements.

Doctor Ricketts said he'd sort me out with a job elsewhere, in a town far, far away from Trevor and his mates, and my constant reminders of Crystal. I catch a glimpse of my reflection in the black of the window and barely recognise myself, just like if I was a fly on the wall this morning. I finish my tea and begin to drift, shoulders relaxed, jaw no longer clenched. And eventually,
I sleep.

On this Occasion

Sitting on one of the fold-down seats next to the doors, you look at the bronze-coloured stitching on your shoes. You follow the arc over your toes, left foot first, then right, and notice the right has an extra stitch. Or maybe the left has one missing; depends on how you look at it, you suppose. You look between your feet at the stain on the carpet. Ribena, maybe? Or blood.

The next stop is Falkirk High.

Regardless of how well the passengers' days are going, the Scotrail robot's mood is consistent whatever the weather. You like its positive lilt, but find it weird that it's often used as well as the guard. You think maybe the guard is for humans only, whereas the robot is exclusively for the non-human: those with expressionless faces, their entire lives plugged into little screens. You look at the woman sitting on the single seat next to the wheelchair-friendly toilet. Like you, she looks lost in routine, bereft of challenge or inspiration.

You look at the little earpiece on your dated mobile. Four tiny holes in hard plastic, like a pepper pot. You'd hoped good news – life-changing news – was going to spring from those holes into your ear . . . But they sent you an email instead. Or maybe it was a robot. The recruitment robot.

Dear Mr Argent, thank you for attending an interview for Project Coordinator. I regret to inform you that on this occasion you have not been successful and therefore your application will not be taken any further at this point. I would, however, encourage you to continue to use your account for future employment opportunities. Yours faithfully, The Recruitment Panel.

The Recruitment Panel. Yet it says 'I' regret to inform you. 'I'. How can a panel of people be one person, you wonder. You consider sending them an email to question this, stating that as a result of their heartless, impersonal rejection and evidently cloudy knowledge of consistent pronoun use, that their decision to not offer you the post was, on this occasion, a fucking blessing in disguise.

But then maybe that'd just be sour grapes.

"Hi there, tickets please," the smiley guard says, a tall, broad-shouldered girl with long, dark hair drawn back in a ponytail. You fumble in the pockets of your suit jacket, then your trousers.

"Sorry about this. It's definitely here somewhere."

"Is that it in your shirt pocket," she points.

"Yes," you say, in a way that sounds like *A-ha, just testing!* "I put it there for handiness, believe it or not. There you go."

"Mind not on it today?" she laughs.

"It'd appear not," you reply, sharing the laughter. "How's your day going?"

"Ach, okay, thanks. Pretty routine stuff, but that's not a bad thing 'cos there can be some crazy trains."

"Like the last trains back to Edinburgh and Glasgow at the weekend?"

"Exactly. Character building though. At least that's what I keep telling myself."

"Do you reckon this is a bloodstain?" You point between your feet.

"Probably. Altercations tend to happen in these bits. Usually drunk folk falling out over something."

"Have you ever had to deal with that kind of stuff?"

"Yeah, a couple of times . . . Other passengers tend to help though, and I've never been hurt. Well, not yet anyway," she laughs. "And hey, at least the money's decent."

"Well, that always helps, doesn't it?"

She gives you back your ticket with the usual squiggle of ink next to the date. "Thank you, enjoy the rest of your day." She walks towards the woman, who's now asleep with her mouth open.

You take off your multi-coloured tie and unbutton the top button of your shirt.

"Tickets please," the guard says loud and clear, but there's no reaction. She gives her shoulder a light shake. "Tickets please."

"Oh my God!" the woman blurts, her arctic eyes wide with fright. "Who the *hell* do you think you are, scaring me like that? I've got a heart condition, you know."

"I woke you as gently as I could, madam. Now, can I see your ticket please?"

"You call that gentle? You brainless bitch! I could've had a heart attack! How dare you! How dare you treat me like this?"

"Can I see your ticket, please?" the guard says again, calmly.

"No you cannot, not after scaring the life out of me like that."

"In that case, I'm afraid I can't permit you to travel, therefore you'll have to get off at the next stop."

Panting pathetically, the woman fumbles in her bag, fishes out a ticket and throws it at the guard. It lands on the tired carpet. The guard reaches down, picks it up and examines it.

169

"This has yesterday's date on it," she says. "You might've pulled the wool over the eyes of the staff at Glasgow Queen Street, but you won't be doing the same with me. Now, where are you going?"

" . . . "

" . . . "

"Polmont."

"Single or return?"

You fold your tie – the tie you wore at your interview – and put it in your suit jacket pocket. You thought it'd tell them that you're approachable; vibrant; energetic. That you like to. Stand out. One of the members of the panel was wearing a similar tie, which you took to be a good sign: like minds working for the same cause.

You wonder what they mean by 'on this occasion'. Is there going to be another occasion where you *will* be successful? Interview 2: The Sequel – This time Johnny Argent gets it right! You could include this in your sour grapes letter, along with challenging what is meant by 'your application will not be taken any further at this point.' So, at which point, you wonder, will it be taken further? But they'd probably use over-complex, drawn-out management jargon to explain that it's a standard response, designed in a way to be gentle with the let-down whilst leaving the door ajar in case the candidate they appointed suddenly has second thoughts, or insists on better terms and conditions, or dies.

Even three days on, your disappointment is still quite deep, which is beginning to grate. You think about what your mum said – 'You know, dear, sometimes they've already got the person handpicked, maybe someone internal, you know, but they still have to go through the motions of advertising it and then interviewing unfortunate souls like yourself. You probably did nothing wrong, dear, I wouldn't worry about it. And at least you've still got a job.'

She had a point. It probably did go to someone internal – someone who's worked there for ages and is in with the director and knows everyone on the team already. You might as well have answered every question with 'no comment' or tore off your shirt, got up on the desk and did *Gangnam Style*, off-key and unbearably loud. You would've enjoyed yourself more and the outcome would've been the same. It'd be great to do something like that, you think to yourself – attend an interview already knowing you have no chance.

"So Mr Argent, the position you've applied for requires a high level of communication and leadership skills. Can you give us an example of how you use such skills in your current post and how you would transfer them to perform this role?"

"Bananas."

"Excuse me?"

"Oh, my apologies, Shaz, I must've picked you up wrongly."

"Shaz?"

"Oh, sorry, but hey, you know, Sharon/Shaz, potato/tomato. Ha ha ha, sorry, what a numpty, I mean potato/potato obvos. Do you prefer Shazza?"

"Mr Argent–"

"Anyway, to answer your question, *Sharon*, no, I wouldn't advise putting the seagull in the blender as that would be an act of animal cruelty, plus you'd have quite a bit of cleaning to do before you could use your blender as a hat again. I know what you're going to say – they're 'vermin' – and whilst I agree, there *are* more appropriate ways of making paint, now aren't there? Does that answer your question?"

"Mr Argent, I'm sorry, but there seems to be a–"

"No need to apologise, darling. But if you feel really bad, you can get up early and make me a nice breakfast. How about kippers? Oh, and remember I like gingerbread syrup in my coffee. Cracking tie by the way, Danny-boy."

"Mr Argent, my name is Daniel and this is entirely inappropriate behavi– "

"Not as inappropriate as your earring, you big poser. Where did you get that? Mothercare?"

"Okay, Mr Argent, that's quite enough, I'm going to ask you to lea–"

"Heeeeeeeeeeyyyyyyyy, sexy laaaaaady, op, op, op, op, oppan Gangnam style. Can I just say, guys, I am, like, really looking forward to working in this team. High five!"

And Mum's right. At least you have a job – which you're good at – which is reasonably well paid – which means you don't have to work weekends. It could be a whole lot worse, like having to deal with a fare dodger or splitting up a drunken fight on a Saturday night train. You reach down and pick at the extra stitch on your right shoe.

Ladies and gentleman, we will shortly be arriving at Falkirk High. Passengers alighting at this station, please ensure to pick up any luggage and personal belongings, and thank you for travelling with First Scotrail.

When you stand up, the fold-down seat flips up and thuds onto the facing. People congregate around you. You like that the announcement was human. The train slows to a halt. You press the illuminated disc and watch the doors open with a lethargic hiss.

This is Falkirk High. The next stop is Polmont.

Today's Weather in Central Scotland

Change
able

Everyone's got their Achilles' Heel

THOMAS WINSTON
0251677
2nd Year BA Business Studies
International Business
Module Lead – Ted Neary

" . . . "
    " . . . "
    " . . . "
    " . . . "

"Eh . . . em . . . hang on, this isn't the right sheet, what have I done with the . . . eh . . ." Thomas pulls other sheets from his pocket. "Right, is this the . . . eh . . . no, that's not it either. Sorry about this. Ah, maybe this is . . . hmm, no." A couple of sheets fall from his grasp. One glides back and forth in the air, feather-like. Head bowed, he laughs nervously, frantically checking the pockets of his jeans and hoodie. "Sorry about this," he says again as his keys clatter to the floor. "Shit." He clamps his hands round his mouth. "Oh, I never meant to say that. Can you erase that on the tape? Oh my God, I can't believe I just said that."

"Stop the tape, Saul," Neary says, hand in the air. "What's the problem, Thomas? This isn't like you."

"I know, I'm sorry, it's just that . . . eh . . . presentations have never really been my strong point. Especially ones that get filmed."

"Okay, just relax and take a deep breath. Saul, can you rewind the tape a bit please – so we can start from scratch. And then maybe you could step outside for a bit, if you don't mind. I'll give you a shout when we're ready to shoot again."

"No problem," Saul says. As the tape whirs back, Thomas paces around in front of the white board, breathing audibly, in through his nose and out through his mouth.

"That's good," Neary says. "Just completely reset yourself."

"I don't think I can do this." Thomas jingles coins in his pocket, one foot moving up and down like he's operating a hi-hat.

"That's it ready to go when you are," Saul says, stepping out of the classroom. Neary sits up in his chair and adjusts his tie.

"I don't understand, Thomas. I've never seen you like this before. You never have a problem talking in class, in front of what, 40-odd classmates?"

"Yeah . . . but this is different. I'm up here instead of in my usual seat and it's just you and Saul . . . and the camera. I just find it totally different." He rubs his neck, hi-hat foot tapping faster.

"Do you think it'd make a difference if the whole class was here?"

"I don't know. Maybe. Or maybe not. No, probably not. Don't think it would make any difference . . . I honestly don't think I can do this."

Neary lifts the marking criteria off the desk. "This is not a difficult assessment, Thomas. All you need to do is tell me what I told the class a couple of weeks ago. Or the notes I handed out at the start of the month – why don't you just paraphrase them? You're perfectly capable."

"Yeah, I remember you saying we'll all pass if we just follow what you said. But the thing is, we *have* to pass this assessment, don't we? And it's not just the subject stuff, it's the presentation side of things too. Like voice and body language and that. That's what it says on the marking criteria."

"Well, yes, that is part of the assessment, but as long as you deliver the information clearly enough, you don't have to concern yourself with that side of things. You'll be fine."

Thomas picks up one of the sheets from the floor. "But it says here that the presentation stuff is split up into . . . eye contact, voice, body language . . . eh, audience engagement . . . appropriateness of slides and, eh . . . professionalism of delivery. So if I don't get at least 40% in each of these, does that mean I fail? And what happens if I fail?"

Neary leans forward. "It's not quite as cut and dried as that. These are just guidelines for what constitutes a good presentation. Like I say, as long as you cover the material we spoke about in class reasonably clearly, you'll pass. It's that simple."

Thomas frowns. "So . . . I don't actually have to be competent in all these areas. Just as long as I'm okay."

"Yes. As long as it's okay, I'll pass you."

"What happens if I'm not okay and I fail?"

"Look, you're not going to fail."

Thomas's frown softens.

"Remember that old Persil advert – PMA." Neary slaps his hand on the desk as he spells out the acronym. "Positive – Mental – Attitude."

178

"But if I do, what will happen to me?"

" . . . "

" . . . "

"You need to pass this assessment to graduate. There's no re-sit. I mentioned that in class last week, remember."

"Oh, God." Thomas claws at his throat, etching two red lines on either side of his Adam's apple. The tempo increases on his hi-hat foot, in tandem with the jingle of coins. Neary places the assessment criteria on the desk, swings back in his seat and scratches his cheek. "I wasn't expecting this," he says. "I thought you would breeze through this assessment."

"Everyone's got their Achilles' Heel," Thomas says, looking at the floor, his shoulders so hunched it looks like he's trying to curl himself into the embryo position.

"I'm sorry, but I can't spend any more time waiting around here. You're going to have to just take a deep breath and go for it."

Thomas breathes like he's pregnant and having contractions. "Can I just . . . ask a question first?"

"Yes, okay."

"What do you mean by an international company? Is that a company that has a presence in, like, more than 50% of the world's countries?"

Neary puts his head in his hands. "Well, what do you think it means? You're a second year degree student, you should know these things by now."

"I'm not 100% sure . . . that's why I'm asking you, sir."

Neary crosses his legs and rests his chin on the heel of his hand. "Look, it's not my job to tell you absolutely everything, and I feel I've given the class sufficient information in order to get through this assessment. What is it about the instructions that you find so difficult?"

"Well . . . it's just that I'm not sure exactly what is meant by an international company . . . and if I get it wrong, well I could fail, and then there's the delivery stuff too. And any time I ask a question, you tell me that I'm a second year degree student and then just give me the question back."

"McDonald's," Neary spouts, holding up his hands. "McDonald's is an international company. Now can we please get on with this?"

Thomas ruffles his hair. A little shower of dandruff falls onto his hoodie. "Okay."

Neary walks to the door and opens it. "You can come back in now, Saul."

He walks back into the classroom and across to the camera. "Righto, ready when you are."

Neary sits down and pulls a biro from the breast pocket of his suit jacket. "Okay, Saul, start the tape."

"Rolling."

"Right, Thomas, whenever you're ready."

Thomas pulls his hood over his head and looks down at the sheet of paper in his hand. Jingling coins in his pocket, he reads from the sheet, word for word, his face growing redder as his voice becomes faster, stumbling over words and phrases as if he's experiencing intermittent electric shocks. He never looks up as he reads about John Lewis, adlibbing how they are similar to McDonald's because they'd like to take over America the way McDonald's has taken over Britain.

"And that's about it," he says, six minutes later, a distinct white line on his jaw from scratching, a line that will become red as his red face returns to white.

"Okay, stop the tape, Saul. And I'm sorry for messing you around, but would you mind stepping outside while I have another word with Thomas?"

"No, not at all." Thomas and Neary watch Saul leave the classroom.

"Did I do enough to pass?"

Neary places his biro on his desk. "Was that honestly the best you could do?"

"Eh, well, yeah. I'm sorry, I just really hate presentations."

"I get that, but no slides?"

"There's one slide," Thomas says, pointing to the blue screen, the yellow letters on it headache-inducing.

"Yes, but it's hardly packed with rich information, is it?"

"Eh, no . . . sorry . . . It's just that I didn't want to be distracted by them. It would've been another thing to remember, another thing to maybe mess up. I know someone who pressed the button and it didn't move on to his next slide, so he pressed it loads of times and then after a few seconds, all the slides just flashed on the screen like it was on fast forward, and then he swore. It was horrible. I just didn't want anything like that to happen to me."

"Okay, here's the deal, Thomas. Your written work is usually of a reasonably good standard and you participate regularly in class. Your presentation was – and I'm sure this is no surprise to you – particularly poor, but under the circumstances I'm willing to give you the benefit of the doubt. I'll award you 40% and we can just forget about this, okay?"

"What about the tape?"

"The tape ran out, or the battery died just after you began and Saul didn't notice."

"Okay," Thomas smiles. "Okay! Great! So I've passed, yeah? I've passed!"

"Yes. Yes you've passed." Neary folds the paperwork and tucks it into his inside pocket.

"You've got to be kidding, right?"

182

"Sorry?"

Thomas pulls down his hood. "I said you've got to be kidding. You're actually going to *pass* me on that? That, what I just did, was terrible. How can *that*, in anyone's book, be a pass?"

"Thomas, what are you—"

"This is an International Business module in a Business Studies degree. My career goal is to work in marketing or public relations for a global business and you honestly think what I've just done successfully fulfills the criteria for a presentation at third year degree level?"

Neary stands up and puts his hands on his hips. "I didn't say it fulfilled the criteria, I *said* I was willing to give you the benefit of the doubt because your written work is good. I'm trying to do you a good turn here, so what's the problem?"

"You're my problem, Ted Neary. Don't think for a moment that your alleged good turn is anything to do with me. You're only trying to protect yourself. You spoon-fed the entire class – *you'll all pass* you said, *you'll all pass*. But why would you spoon-feed us? Because if everyone passes then you look great, don't you? 100% success rate! Wow, what a teacher! Giving me a pass tells me I'm a competent presenter and can transfer that competence to what? An interview? A room full of clients waiting to invest? You must be having a laugh."

Neary, expressionless apart from a slight frown, puts his hands in his pockets and hooks his thumbs into his belt latches. Thomas, now fidget-free, stands tall with his shoulders back.

"I'm on to you, Ted. You would happily point the finger at Saul for the battery on the camera dying, write up a set of notes that justify a borderline pass and then pull the wool over the external's eyes by using my written work as evidence of competency. But an interview isn't something I can write, is it? Nor can I give clients pieces of paper and refuse to talk to them, can I? You don't give a toss what happens to me – or anyone else for that matter – as long as we do what you say so your stats look good. But what about our 'university experience', as the union calls it? Eh? Don't you get paid to inspire us? Encourage us? Make sure we've got the skills we need to be successful in the business world? All you do is tell us exactly what we need to know for the assessments and that we'll all pass. And any time anyone asks a question, you just bounce it back, probably because you don't know even the answer yourself."

"I do that to encourage self-directed learning," Neary says in a monotone.

"I'm ignoring that comment because that's what it deserves. Now here's the deal – the tape malfunctions so all evidence of the presentations is lost, meaning we all have to do them again. You set a task that is appropriate for our level and give us starting points instead of spoon-feeding. You get someone in to do a presentation skills workshop, maybe a guest speaker from industry, and you have another member of staff in the room during the presentations, who helps decide the marks. Finally, if any of us has a question, you either give us an answer that *encourages* self-directed learning or have the decency to admit that you don't know, but you'll look into it. No bouncing back because it doesn't suit your criteria. Have we got a deal?"

Neary removes his hands from his pockets and applauds. "Great performance, Thomas, that's totally made my day." His laugher becomes heartier as his applause becomes louder and faster. Thomas laughs along, mimicking his sarcasm until Neary gets fed up and stops.

"Look, son, don't think for a second you can threaten me. I've been here 25 years, you know. *I'm* the one who makes the rules round here, not you. There will be no reassessment and your 40% stands. Now get out of my face."

"In that case, I'll be going to your line manager and the Students' Union. There's no way I'm letting someone like you, who gets paid, what, 45 grand a year, get away with what you're doing and have the nerve to call it teaching."

"Ha! But it's your word against mine. You don't have a leg to stand on, Thomas, now get out of my classroom and stop wasting my time." Neary shakes his head and laughs.

Thomas walks across to the camera and pulls his iPhone off the side of it, which Saul had stuck on with Velcro.

"My evidence is right here, Neary." Thomas shakes the iPhone like it's a jar of sweeties.

"Nice try, son, but that's breach of university policy. You didn't ask if you could record me."

"Neither did you. And I don't see anything in the guidelines. So, what's it going to be?"

Like, Billions

There was this guy I used to work with, right, and he kept telling me he had loads of great ideas, like loads and loads, right, but because he had a family, right, he had to work long hours, like, to pay the mortgage, 'cos he had a nice big house and it needed to be warm, right, so he had to work even longer hours when the fuel bills went up, right, even though the companies made, like, billions, right, and all the time he just wanted to write or, like, act or direct or that, like bring stories to life, right, but he needed the warm house for his family, and the bills got higher and higher, right, and he never had time to do anything with his ideas, so he got really, really annoyed one day, right, and, like, totally lost the plot, short fuse, big bang and that, right, had to go off with stress and then died of a heart attack at 54, right, having done nothing with all his ideas, right, which were brilliant, right, or at least the ones he told me about in the canteen were, and that's just not right, right, and his poor wife and kids, right, and the bills got higher and higher, right, and the fuel companies' profits got higher and higher, right, and the bills got higher and higher, right, and the fuel companies' profits got higher and higher, right, and the bills got higher and higher, right.

Peaches 'n' Cream

I press my tongue hard onto the side of my tooth. As the victim is struck by his assailant, I press harder, levering to uproot, dismissive of the odds against the fleshy mass getting any purchase. He falls to the ground and is kicked hard. For every boot, I lever harder and the nerve rages.

Trying to make up time, the bus driver races over a sleeping policeman, rattling his passengers around like Tic-Tacs. My book falls to the floor. People around me tut and sigh. A teenager says 'fuck's sake'. I reach down to pick it up. The nerve begins its recovery from persistent invasion.

Before I can find my page, the bus reaches its final destination. Someone rings the bell and I clock the driver frowning in his mirror. The doors open. Passengers file down the aisle, me at the rear, still looking for my page.

"Was that you who rung that bell?" snaps the driver.

"No," I say, raising my book to my throat. "I don't know who it was."

"Pisses me off when folk do that. I mean, I'm obviously going to stop at the bloody bus station, amn't I?"

I flick my tongue rapidly off my tooth. It's a different sensation than when I press.

"Eh, yeah," I say.

I step off the bus, flicking away, the tip of my tongue prickling. I don't look back at the driver. The doors close and he drives alongside me like a kerb-crawler. My tongue finds extra strength and the nerve throbs, nearing the border between dull and moderate pain. The driver pulls up at another stance where there's a queue of people. I weave through them and head for town.

On my way to the dentist, I see Charley Samson, who's gorgeous. I think back to high school and cringe at the day I told my pals she was frigid. I only did it 'cos I was scared. No wonder she dumped me. The nerve aches and the flesh on my tongue is beginning to tear. Once she passes, I look at my watch. Early. I sit on a bench and rest. I want boiled sweets for comfort – Peaches 'n' Cream, like my mum used to give me in my lunch box, but it's too much of such comforts that got me here in the first place. So I close my eyes and just breathe.

I feel woozy after the dentist. I lean on a handrail at my stance and look at my watch. Early. I find my page and begin to read. The assailant pours diesel over his victim. It goes in his mouth and he chokes. I push my tongue into the gap. He lights a match and lets go. The victim ignites, his flesh burning as the flames lick his assailant's shoes. I flick and ram and press and push, but there's only numbness. The bus pulls up and the doors hiss like an angry snake. I look up to see the same bus driver. My tongue automatically does what it does. I miss my tooth.

Mind, at the end of Primary 6

"I remember being really excited," Andy says, looking through the window.

"Me too," says Fraser. "I couldn't wait until the bell rang. I told my mum about it the night before and she said 'Really? They're going to let you and your classmates walk into town yourselves at lunchtime – primary 6s – on their own!'"

"Crazy when you think about it, eh? Teachers letting kids cross busy roads to go to fuckin' McDonald's for their lunch. That kind of thing would be on the news these days."

A guy sitting at a window table looks up through the glass.

"Just look at the amount of shit on that table," Fraser says. "Two Big Macs, two of those little cheeseburgers, two cokes and two McFlurrys. I wonder how many calories are in that lot?"

"Fuckin' hundreds, man . . . It's weird though – *we* were that little boy on that day at the end of primary 6," Andy points. "Remember the buzz on the way there?"

"Totally."

"Everyone talking about what they were going to get, how much money their mums had given them, if they were going to go large or just get regular."

"Yeah, and remember fat Harry Gillespie's mum gave

him enough for a Big Mac, a McChicken Sandwich *and* a milkshake? He was the envy of the school that day."

Frowning, the dad mouths 'What?' His son hasn't even noticed Andy and Fraser, his mouth busy chomping away at beefy cardboard and hot lettuce on ketchup-sodden baps.

"I'd love to go in there and give him grief for feeding his kid a load of rubbish," Andy says. "I mean, what kind of meal is that to give your kid at Easter time?"

"He probably can't cook, man. Too busy working or something. You know what it's like these days."

"You sound like an old bastard talking like that," Andy laughs.

"Well I am 25 years older than I was the day we went to this very restaurant, running about like it was Christmas or something."

"Don't call it a restaurant, man. Restaurants serve food."

Walking down the high street, Fraser nearly steps in vanilla milkshake on the ground. "Looks like someone didn't quite make it to the bin,"

"And they were soooooo close too," Andy says, picking up the cup, lid and straw. "Maybe they mistook the middle of the high street for the bin."

"Well, yeah, maybe. Easy mistake to make after all," Fraser says.

When they arrive at the old Tesco car park, there's hardly anybody around. A couple of guys have just turned the corner to head down the hill towards Lidl, leaving only Andy, Fraser and the guys in JCBs working on the new KFC building. They walk towards the metal fence and look closer at the shell behind it. Attached to the fence with cable ties is a couple of notices. One says Keep Out and the other displays information about the project and the names of the managers.

"What is it with Scottish towns wanting to be American?" Fraser says, shaking his head.

"Fuck knows," Andy says. "Popularity maybe?"

"But how did shit food and creepy, paedo-looking mascots become so popular the world over? I mean, just pretend there was no KFC or McDonald's, right?"

"Right."

"And me and you decided to open a fast food joint selling high fat, low nutrition junk at low prices."

"Uh-huh."

"And then I suggest we get a couple of mascots to attract children, to make the food more 'fun'. For the chicken, the floating head of a Rolf Harris look-a-like, and for the burgers, a clown like the one from Stephen King's *IT*, who plays and laughs with the kids and gives them junk food and toys in a box, which we'll call a Happy Meal."

Andy snorts.

"Do you think it would take off? And that all across the world, our corporate logo would be recognised by everyone – and I mean EVERYONE."

"Oh, come on, man, at least the Burger King in the high street has closed down," Andy says.

"And what's Burger King not got?" Fraser turns, eyes wide.

"A creepy mascot?"

"Exactly!"

"But at least it's one less."

"True. But how many fast food joints do you think there are in Falkirk?"

Andy looks to the sky, doing a quick count in his head. "Just Falkirk? Or Camelon and Polmont and that too?"

"Camelon, Polmont, Bainsford, Larbert. Surrounding areas."

"Hmmmm, about 30?"

"72," Fraser says. "So what I want to know is – why does Falkirk Council think we need a KF fuckin' C Drive-Thru?"

Andy says nothing, just shakes his head and looks through the fence, eyes narrow. One of the JCB guys stops what he's doing and looks over. Andy and Fraser stare back until the JCB starts moving again.

"72 fast food joints and only one book shop – or two if you count the Christian one on Glebe Street. You know, you can't even buy a CD in this town any more, unless it's from a supermarket," Fraser says, taking his mobile phone out of his pocket.

"What are you doing?" Andy asks.

"Putting the number of the Construction & Safety Manager in my phone." Once he's punched in the number, he puts his phone back in his pocket, pulls out a penknife and flips the blade. The same JCB guy stops what he's doing and looks over again.

"Bloody joke, isn't it?" comes a voice from behind them.

Andy and Fraser turn to see a tall guy in an orange boiler suit and white skip cap walking towards them, carrying a black rubbish bag and a grabber.

"What, this place?" Andy says.

"Yeah. I'll tell you what'll happen. All those fat bastard bus drivers over there" – he points towards the bus station with his grabber – "will all come here for their lunches and dinners and just end up fatter. And at night, there'll be queues of cars lining up for the drive-thru, booming like mobile discos, and then they'll just chuck their litter out the window. And who'll have to pick it up? ME! This town's getting dirtier and dirtier 'cos of shitholes like this." He jabs the air with his grabber towards the shell. The guy in the JCB lifts a mobile phone to his ear.

"You're right, man," Andy says. "Nobody seems to give a horse's arse though."

"You'd probably be better eating a horse's arse than some of the shite they'll be selling in there," the litterpicker says. "They aren't even allowed to call it Kentucky Fried Chicken anymore 'cos their products don't contain enough chicken. They can call the wings and drumsticks chicken 'cos it's on the bone, and that pulled chicken they've been advertising, but look out for adverts for the tower burger or the zinger thingamyjig – no mention of the word chicken 'cos it's illegal if there isn't a certain percentage of chicken in it. And folk will be queuing up in their droves for it too. Makes me sick."

"No mention of Kentucky either," Andy says. "I wonder what Kentucky think about that."

"If I was Kentucky, I'd be happy," Fraser says, stroking his blade, the sun reflecting off it. "You know, I hadn't noticed that about the tower burgers."

"Full of additives and derivatives," the litterpicker says, picking a cigarette butt off the pavement with his grabber. He takes off his cap and wipes his forehead with his sleeve. "You know, if you leave a zinger burger lying out, it takes months to perish. What does that tell you, eh? Any fresh food starts to perish as soon as it's unwrapped or left out the fridge. But not this crap. I'll tell you, whoever it was at the council that gave this the go ahead deserves to be threatened with that blade there . . . Oh-ho, here we fuckin' go again." He points at the guy getting out the JCB and walking towards them. "I'm out of here."

"See you later, pal," Andy says. Fraser takes a small cloth for polishing specs out of his pocket and wipes the blade and handle of the penknife.

"Alright lads," JCB guy says, approaching the fence.

"Yeah," Andy and Fraser say in unison.

"Do you two know that guy?"

"What, that guy we were just talking to?" Andy says.

"Yeah, him there," he points. "With the ram on the back of his overall. Lenny Ingram. He's a volunteer litterpicker."

"I've seen him about," Fraser says. "Didn't know he was a volunteer though, or that his name was Lenny. Is there a problem, like?"

"What's your business here?" he asks, taking off his hardhat to reveal a thick head of dark hair, peppered grey. "You've been standing here a while now, just looking."

"It's not a crime," Andy says. "We're just interested in building sites."

"Fair enough, but what's with the knife?"

"We're photographers," Fraser says, polishing the handle with his cloth. "I'm pleased you came over actually. We're doing a night class at the college and we've to take photos of the sun reflecting off something in a local location. Lots of folk in our class are taking pictures of the Kelpies, but we want to be a bit different, so I thought we'd take some shots of the sun reflecting off a switchblade with the building site for the new KFC in the background, but out of focus, you know, kind of blurry. Thought it might look quite arty."

"Arty and sinister, like the front cover of a crime novel or something," Andy says. "We're just waiting for the sun to get a bit brighter, so that's why we're hanging around. Have a look at the knife if you want, it's not that sharp. We aren't here to cause trouble."

Fraser passes it through the fence. "So, is it alright with

you if we use the site as a background, or do you want me to give your manager a bell first? I've put his number in my phone."

JCB looks at the knife. His expression softens. "I don't see any cameras."

"Andy here has the best iPhone on the market. It's as good as any camera if you know what you're doing."

JCB passes the knife back through the fence, runs a hand through his hair and puts his hardhat back on. "It's alright with me. As long as none of the workmen are in it."

"No probs," Fraser says.

They watch him walk back and climb into his JCB.

"I'm embarrassed," Andy says.

"About what?"

"Mind, at the end of primary 6: the excitement about McDonald's. Total cringe."

"Don't worry about it. I used to think Noel Gallagher was a lyrical genius. Tomorrow never knows what it doesn't know too soon. Like, what the fuck does that even mean?"

"Ha! Fuck knows!"

"Right, are you ready?"

Andy has a quick look around. "Yeah, let's go."

When JCB hears the ring of feet on the fence, he jumps out his cabin and runs. But by the time he reaches them, they've already handcuffed themselves to one of the struts.

"What the hell are you two doing?"

"You need to stop working," Fraser shouts. "Stop turning our town into a great big advert for fast food."

"Are you stupid or something? Don't you think we've got the tools to cut through those cuffs?" JCB laughs.

"This isn't about you, man, we're only looking after the town. But if you want to make this personal," Fraser takes his phone out his pocket with his free hand "I can phone your manager and tell him you threatened us with a penknife. Your fingerprints are all over it."

The Saviour

The beady eyes of the life-sized black dogs stare over their fenced enclosure as you regularly adjust your position to get comfortable. No-one else is in the waiting room – except the receptionist who's sitting on a raised stool behind an oak counter. You want to ask her what happened to her arm.

The terracotta walls have certificates on them. Next to reception a cork board, over-populated with thank-you cards, hangs slightly squint. Directly across from you, above a row of empty seats, are two paintings. One is a watercolour of withered sunflowers baking in heat, the other a portrait of a woman. Her eyes are wide as if she's looking at something scary. Her brown hair flicks up from her black polo-neck.

Apart from the sound of the receptionist leafing through a magazine, the room is silent. The strong smell of pot pourri is making you feel a little nauseous. You admire the paintwork on the black dogs' enclosure and are drawn back to their faces. They're agitated at being fenced in, keen to explore what's beyond the walls of the clinic. *The Back Clinic*. A beautiful manor house partially converted into a surgery.

"I didn't know this place existed until I heard the advert on the radio."

The receptionist looks up, alarmed. You look into her eyes and then at the portrait. Different hair, a bit heavier and no cast, but it's the same person.

"Oh, that's good then," she says. "I didn't think that advert was worth the money to be honest, so it's good to hear it's at least working a little bit."

She looks down at her magazine and thumbs back a page.

"Yeah . . . And I only live up the road, too. Must've walked past this place a thousand times."

"Probably the trees." She glances up and then back to her magazine. "The trees hide the sign. We really need to get them trimmed."

"Ah, right."

" . . . "

" . . . "

You run the back of your hand across your brow and flinch as the muscles in your lower back remind you why you're here. The dogs seem closer, the shine of the porcelain brighter.

"Tell me." You lean forward slightly. "Do his patients really call him The Saviour? Or was that just something he said to make the advert funny?"

"No, it's true," she replies. "It was a woman from America. She read the website and decided to travel over to see what he could do – and he cured her. While she was here she spread the word to the locals, referring to him as The Saviour. There was a bit in the paper about it, a couple of months ago."

"Oh, I didn't see that." You assume it's not the first time she's told the story.

You look at the portrait again and wonder if her eyes were purposely made bigger. She now has a fringe, which covers her right eye. You think the fringe and different make-up make her left eye appear smaller, or certainly less obvious.

"Hope you don't mind me asking," you say. She looks up and twitches. "But what happened to your arm?"

"Mr Fullerton?" The Saviour emerges from wooden double doors. You squint at his outline, the sun's rays shooting at you from behind him. He steps forward to reveal his coarse face, eyes set back in his skull like crevasses in a mountain range.

"Yes." You carefully lever yourself from your chair. You look at his brown sandals, grey trousers and knee-length white lab coat as you straighten.

"Would you like to come through?"

He stands to the side and extends an arm. You glance at the portrait and walk into the sunlight. As he closes the doors, you swear you can hear the dogs snarl.

Up at the Lock-ups

"But isn't Joey Simm only five?"

"Yeah, but seriously, he can do wheelies for, like, ever!" Ralph says. "C'mon, you really need to see this."

"Just give me a minute, my trainers are upstairs. Here, have a gobstopper." Dougie throws Ralph a small, crumpled white bag. Ralph fishes around and picks out a red one. He always avoids the green ones as they taste like washing-up liquid.

"Right, let's go!" Dougie thunders down the stairs, his brand new Adidas Sambas tied tight, the white toes virginal and bright. "I'm away out, Mum!"

"Okay, but mind and be back at six for your tea," Dougie's mum shouts from the living room.

Ralph and Dougie walk up Finestere Avenue – past old Jean's, who always gives them selection boxes at Christmas time; past Kris and Yolanda's, who used to take them ice skating with their daughter, Jade, until she had the tip of her pinky sliced off by another skater; and past Mrs Tierney's hedges, cut into the shapes of ducks and swans, surrounded by colourful flowers.

"Wait for it," Ralph says. And even though they know what to expect, they both still jolt with fright when the Thomson's collie-cross, Shadow, growls from the other side of the gnawed fence, his bared teeth jutting through a gap between the posts. The boys up their pace as jets of foam shoot onto the pavement.

"Poor mutt," Ralph says once they're past the Thomson's, walking by Rocco's clapped out old Ford Capri.

"There's a bit of a nip in that wind now we're coming into autumn," Dougie says, hunching his shoulders, zipping his tracksuit top right up to his neck.

"Ha ha, you sound like an OAP talking like that. *Mind and wrap up now, son, you'll catch your death out there,*" Ralph mocks, a pink slaver escaping the corner of his mouth, drawing a perfect line to his jaw, like a faded slash wound.

"Yeah, well, you're the one dribbling like you're in a nursing home. It's called a gobstopper for a reason."

A crowd of people has gathered at the lock-ups, some swigging Irn Bru and eating crisps, others trying discreetly to drink cider from blue plastic bottles. The doors of the lock-ups are different colours, some chipped and rusting, others well looked after. Joey Simm, smiling, with floppy ginger hair covering his forehead, sits on a little beige-coloured bike to the left of number 8, the first in the row.

"Right, do it again, little guy, but further this time," Davey Wells says. "Do you think you could do the full length of the lock-ups?"

"All eleven of them?" Joey Simm squeaks.

"Yeah." Davey's eyes are big, his forehead furrowed.

Ralph and Dougie nestle themselves into the crowd and clock Davey whispering to the guys around him, their hands quickly exchanging notes.

"What do I get if I do it?" Joey Simm asks.

"How about . . . a Mars Bar?"

His ears prick up like a dog being told it's dinner time.

"Sure," he cheeps, positioning his pedals.

208

Dougie notices Billy Watson appear from the path that leads to the woods. He's on his BMX, chewing gum; face scrunched like a discarded crisp packet.

"Bet I can do it as well," Billy grunts. Everyone looks round. "And if I do, I'll be expecting some of that." He nods towards Davey's hands. "*And* some of that." He nods towards Sparky Green's bottle of cider.

" . . . "
" . . . "

"Yeah, okay," Davey says, scanning the crowd, their contempt for Billy and his reputation in the street obvious. Billy positions himself next to Joey Simm, right pedal raised, poised to go, as if it's a serious competition. Ralph and Dougie notice a few more hands exchanging notes.

"Okay, little man, after three," Davey says. "One . . . twooooo . . . . . three!"

Joey Simm takes off at lightning speed, his front wheel off the ground before Billy knows where he is. Flummoxed, Billy puts in extra effort. Dougie and Ralph look at each other and laugh.

"Go on yourself, little guy!" Davey shouts.

"You can do it," Sparky Green slurs, raising a flimsy fist in the air.

"Go, Joey, go!"

As he glides past the third lock-up, Billy pushes himself and gains a bit of ground. The crowd counts in chorus as Joey Simm races towards glory . . . and a Mars Bar.

"SIX . . . SEVEN . . . EIGHT . . . NINE . . ."

Billy, getting closer, now only one lock-up behind, gives a final push.

"TEN . . ."

He falls backwards and crashes onto the tarmac. His BMX lands on top of him.

"ELEVENNNN!"

But Joey Simm keeps going, front wheel raised, pedaling hard down Finestere Avenue, maybe thinking it could get him another Mars Bar. Billy wriggles on the ground, squealing, clutching his elbow. People cheer and clap and laugh, even those who have lost money. No-one goes to see if Billy is okay.

"Look!" Dougie shrieks. And those not looking already turn to see Joey Simm, still pulling the perfect wheelie, whizzing down Finestere Avenue as Shadow whizzes up.

Hard to Start

Oh I should also tell you
Even though Ernest has been a farmer all his life he sometimes has
difficulty dealing with stillborn lambs or those that die after birth
Puts pressure on himself to get 100%
Probably because he's been a farmer so long he sees it as failure to
get anything less
We got 100% four years ago but lost quite a few last year
He'll be wanting to make up for it this year I expect
Just so you know in case the conversation comes up

Anyway looking forward to meeting you when you arrive
Let me know if the directions to the farm make sense
You can always give me a ring if you get lost
although mobile reception is really patchy up here.
Sometimes we have nothing for days even if the weather's fine
Same with the TV so you're probably best recording anything you
watch regularly
See you soon

Kind Regards
Sandra Clayworth

Greer-Ridge Farm
Suppliers of fresh, local produce

*

"Ernest, this is our new helper, Roy. Roy, this is Ernest."

"Call me Ernie," he says, standing up from the kitchen table, hand extended. "Ernest sounds so old fashioned, doesn't it? My old boy's fault, really," he laughs.

I shake his hand. "Nice to meet you, Ernie. Lovely farm you've got here."

"That's thanks to this little one," he says, patting Sandra's bum.

"Ernest!" She blushes. "It's all the oxytocin in the air at this time of year," she tells me. "What do you take in your tea, Roy?"

"Just milk, please."

"What, no tea?" Ernie laughs, slapping the table.

"This milk is ours," Sandra says, lifting a white jug. "Fresh produce from only metres away."

"Brilliant," I say with a smile.

"Please, sit down, Roy," Ernie says, gesturing to the chair across from him. I take a seat and admire the pink and white checked tablecloth and cattle-themed placemats. From the fridge, Sandra produces a stacked plate of sandwiches and places them in the centre of the table.

"I was only expecting a cup of tea, this is great." I say.

"You'll need your energy," Ernie says, "because we're going out in *that*." He points to the window at the rain powering down from the sky. I think back a couple of hours, driving through the hills, my windscreen wipers working so hard I thought they were going to fly off.

"It's okay. I brought two sets of waterproofs and two pairs of wellies, just in case."

"Bloody good job," Ernie laughs, showing some partially chewed sandwich. "When was the last time you were on a farm?"

"Must be nearly ten years now," I say. "I'd be about 12

or 13, but I loved it. So when I saw your ad for a helper, I jumped at the chance."

"You'll have a good time up here. Most people do."

Ernie is the stereotypical farmer – slightly overweight, but tall and muscular with a weather-beaten face and thinning grey hair. Sandra is petite, although a little top-heavy, with a dyed brown bob, purple rimmed glasses and a smile that tells me she hasn't got a bad bone in her body. I had read online that they were a friendly and welcoming couple, but sitting at their table, I felt like I was in a kid's storybook.

"Okay, so there's ham, lettuce & mustard and smoked salmon & cream cheese. Please, help yourself, Roy," Sandra says.

"Thanks, these look magic." I lift two of each and place them on my plate.

"Homemade bread as well," Ernie says. "She keeps me well this one, Roy."

"She certainly does," I say. "These are delicious."

"And there's refrigerator cake for afters," Sandra says.

"When did you make that?" Ernie asks.

"I didn't. It was Nora. She brought it over last night when you were out checking the sheep."

"She's a gem, that girl. An absolute gem."

"Nora's our niece," Sandra says. "She lives in the next village."

"I love refrigerator cake."

"Wait till you taste *this* one," Ernie says. "Honestly, Nora's refrigerator cake is the best."

"There's none for you, Ernest," Sandra says, winking at me.

"Wh . . . wh . . . whaaaat?" Ernie holds his chest, mimicking a heart attack, then bursts into laughter.

Half an hour later, dressed head to toe in waterproofs and filled to the gunnels with Nora's refrigerator cake, Ernie and I are out in the Bush Hog, buzzing about the fields and checking the sheep, looking for any about to give birth. The farm's sheepdog, Jess, is in the cage in the back, unperturbed by the heavy rain, taking everything in her stride. The sky, despite the downpour, is bright, a combination almost spiritual, if not a little eerie.

"Look out for ones a bit away from the herd. Sometimes they lie down. Or you might see a sort-of red and blue sac hanging out the back of them. That's amniotic fluid. Means the lamb's coming," Ernie says, avoiding a deep muddy puddle.

I can barely hear him over the noise of the engine.

"What does this thing run on?"

"What?"

"The Hog. What does it run on?" I ask again, raising my voice.

"Red Diesel. Or used vegetable oil."

"Ah, right. Handy little vehicle, isn't it?"

"Beats walking around the fields in this." Ernie points to the sky. "That's what we had to do back in the day."

"Jeezo, I don't fancy that at all."

"My old boy used to say you're not a man until you've done lambing season with no more than your dog and your crook."

"We take a lot for granted these days, don't we?"

"We do. But this is a great little thing," Ernie says, patting the steering wheel. "I can have the dog in the back, carry meds for any sheep that are sick, transport a sheep from one field to another if I need to, or back to the byres."

"Why would you take a sheep back to the byres?"

"Sometimes they reject their young, so you need to take the lamb and its mother back to the byre so they can bond, and the lamb can be fed properly. If you just leave them in the field to sort themselves out, the lamb could die from neglect. It tends to only happen with gimmers."

"Gimmers?"

"Yeah, first time mothers."

"Ah."

Ernie stops and gets out to open the gate into the next field, but when he comes back, he comes to my side. I open the door.

"Hop over then," he says, getting in, giving me no choice. "Have you driven an automatic before? Or a dodgem?"

"Yeah, both," I laugh.

"Good, well this is just as easy."

He quickly talks me through what to do and soon enough I'm driving across the field, checking every sheep for anything out of the ordinary.

"There's one," Ernie shouts, the sudden sound making me momentarily accelerate. I regain control and drive towards it slowly.

"Stop about five or six metres away," he says. "This one's a gimmer."

"Do you want me to do anything?" I ask.

"That's why you're here, plus your knees are much younger than mine," he smiles. "Out you get."

We put up our hoods and get out. The rain drums off my waterproofs so intensely, it's like it's trying to push me into the ground like a tent peg. Ernie lets Jess out of the back and she immediately stands to heel.

"Okay, on you go, girl."

She circles the panicked sheep, narrowing its potential

escape routes. Having only ever seen a sheepdog at work on TV, it's exciting watching it happen for real, and for a purpose, not just to impress judges and win awards for their owners.

"Take this," Ernie says, handing me his crook, "and when I say *now*, run towards the sheep and hook it under its throat."

We stand in the teeming rain, still and quiet, watching Jess do what she does best. I feel like I'm in the blocks for the 100 metre sprint, waiting for a gun to sound. My eyes flit between Jess and the sheep, my grip tight on the crook, hands soaking from rainwater dripping off my cuff.

"Now!"

I dart out the blocks and nearly fall flat on my face, but I manage to correct myself and race towards the sheep. When I completely miss its head with the crook and it falls from my grasp, my instincts make me dive, like a wrestler, my mind somehow switched off to the fact I'm throwing myself at a sheep in labour. It's suddenly all about me and for a moment, as I'm careering through the air, I feel stupid, but it passes as soon as I've got the sheep's wool between my fingers, gripping it tight. It struggles wildly, bleating in dismay. I manage to pull it to the ground and roll it onto its back so it can't move. Jess continues to circle. The amniotic sac from the sheep's back end flops around on my left shin and, through the rain and bleating, I hear Ernie approaching.

"Different!" he laughs, "but just as effective I suppose. Okay, roll her onto her side and let's see what we've got here."

I carefully roll her over and Ernie restrains her.

"Put Jess back in the Hog. Go on, Jess. Go on, girl!"

"Come, Jess," I shout, and although she only met me about an hour ago, she obeys. I don't even have to give a command for her to jump back into the cage.

"Good girl." I shut the door and head back to Ernie. As soon as I can focus through the rain, I see him pull a lamb from the gimmer.

"Wow." I stand still, open-mouthed.

Ernie sticks his fingers into the lamb's mouth. "Got to make sure there's nothing blocking its airway," he says, pulling out strings of mucus and shaking it off his hand. "A few years ago, I had two sheep having twins at the same time – see the sheep marked blue?"

"Uh-huh," I say, looking across the field.

"They're the ones expecting twins. Anyway, one of the lambs died because its bloody airway was blocked. Can't let that happen again." Ernie stands the lamb up. "This little fella looks pretty good though . . . There we go, young'n," he says. "Go and see your mummy."

Shaky on its feet and bleating loudly, the lamb totters towards its mother. Grinning, Ernie stands up and takes a few steps back so they can come together. I don't know why, but I decide to look at the sky. Bullets of rain hit my eyes and I flinch like I've been stung by a wasp. When my vision returns and my brain registers that I'm in a field in the middle of nowhere, watching a sheep licking womb lining and pink gunge off its newborn, I feel privileged – honoured even – to have been a part of it.

"Right, they'll be fine. 100% record maintained. Let's move on to the next field."

Hours later, once we've been round every field twice and are content that the sheep are either fine or not yet ready to give birth, we head back to the farmhouse, where Sandra has been preparing a roast chicken dinner.

After eating enough for two, I go up to my room and unpack my things. Once my case is empty, I lie down on the kingsize bed and watch the rain pound off the Velux window. Only a couple of sheets of glass stand between my now completely dry face and the downpour that soaked it. I laugh, realising that such a thought wouldn't even cross my mind if it was a standard window. It's the perspective that's somehow amusing, not the act of rain striking glass. Then I wonder why I'm thinking about it in so much depth, or at all, and I laugh louder, but this time when my laughter fades, I can feel myself drift – so I pick up my phone from the bedside table to set my alarm. 1 new message. Kristina.

> I know ur away jst now + was in 2 minds about whether to mssg u but Cooper has been in a car crash + is in v bad shape

I read it quickly, but I'm so tired my brain only has the capacity to deal with setting the alarm before I fall asleep.

At 5.30am, I fumble around in the bedclothes to silence the muffled alarm. It takes me a few seconds to get my bearings, but once I realise where I am, I have to fight the urge to press the snooze button. I reluctantly swing my legs over the side of the bed, rest my feet on the floor and rub my face to start my engine. There's a difference in the quality of the air I'm breathing. I hadn't noticed it yesterday, maybe because it was gradual and there were lots of distractions. Here, I've just woken from a deep, peaceful sleep and looked out of the window to the farm, the sheep like little balls of cotton wool, the rain gone, the sky blue. No intense city hubbub, no throb of traffic or bustle of people, just birdsong and the distant bleating of sheep and lambs, some less than a day old. I quite quickly feel fresh, excited at what the day could bring. All the life out there on the farm. All the new life that was going to join it. And then, just as I'm about to spring to my feet to get dressed, I remember my sister's text. Car crash + is in v bad shape. I look at the text again then press reply, but there's no signal.

Cooper's one of the nicest guys I've ever met. Went to primary school with him so I've known him most of my life, although I haven't seen him for ages, not since he met Stacey and stopped coming to the football. I try not to think about what's happened. People survive car crashes all the time, I tell myself. It'll be a scare, a wake-up call. He'll be sore for a bit, confidence knocked and all that. But he'll be fine. He'll be fine.

"Come on, give us another kiss," I hear Ernie say as I make my way along the hall to the kitchen, the door a fraction ajar. "You're a bit ticklish this morning, aren't you?"

Sandra's voice goes up an octave. "No, Ernest, no! Don't you dare!"

Slippers shuffle on linoleum. Plates and cups chink as Ernie chases her round the table, the pair of them giggling and grunting, like cartoon farm animals.

"Got ye!" Ernie cries in celebration. "Now give me that kiss, you lovely little thing."

Their lips smack together through the laughter and then, I assume because he's squeezed her bum, she squeals.

"Ernest! Stop it! You'll wake Roy!"

"Sorry, what was that? Think you've deafened me a little there," he laughs. "And everyone within a five mile radius."

They're breathy as their laughter subsides. "You're a frisky old devil today, aren't you, Ernest Clayworth? Wasn't last night enough for you?"

"Morning," I say, walking in. Their faces are a picture,

like a teenage son caught by his mother looking at porn. "Oxytocin?"

"Ah, morning, Roy . . . Sleep well? Bed comfy enough for you? What would you like for breakfast? I can grill you some sausages if you like. Sit down and I'll make us a fresh pot of tea."

Ernie grins at me and nods as Sandra busies herself with her back to us, filling the kettle and washing out the teapot. "We're just celebrating how well lambing season's gone this year," he says.

"Yes . . . yes, that's right. But it's not quite over yet," Sandra says.

"We're on the home straight though," Ernie says. "No reason why we can't get 100% this year. No reason at all. And look at the weather." He points out the kitchen window. "You're certainly getting a flavour for how unpredictable it can be up here, Roy. You know, when we're done tonight, we might even have a strong enough TV signal to watch *Match of the Day*. Do you like a bit of the beautiful old game, Roy?"

"Yeah, of course."

"Don't count your chickens though," Sandra says, turning round, her face mellowed to a pitted pink. "Good weather doesn't mean a good signal. Remember we tried to watch a bit of the Wimbledon final last year? The sun was splitting the skies, but the picture kept freezing. And then just the other week when it was raining like it was yesterday, we managed to get through an entire film. Lot of rubbish though, wasn't it, Ernest? Nothing but men shooting each other. I don't understand why some people find that entertaining."

"I didn't think it was that bad," Ernie says. "Escapism they call it, my dear. Escapism."

After sausages, fried eggs and toast, and several mugs

of tea, Ernie and I step into our wellies and head out onto the farm. Behind one of the byres, there's a big metal contraption I've only ever seen on TV.

"Feeding time for the sheep," he says, attaching a polythene sack to the end of a chute. He pulls a chain, which reminds me of the flush on old fashioned toilets, the ones with a high cistern, and the bag quickly fills with grain.

"I thought sheep just ate grass," I say.

"They need this as well," Ernie says, tying the sack and preparing another bag. "Especially pregnant ewes. There's protein in this stuff, you see, cottonseed meal they call it, and vitamins and minerals too. They need the nutrients to make sure they're healthy. Grass only does so much."

"I see."

"And if the ewe's healthy then there's every chance the lamb will be too. But I'll tell you," – he pulls the chain – "whether they're male, female, pregnant or not pregnant, they bloody love this stuff." He places the second bag next to the first and walks away. "Well, aren't you coming?"

"What about the grain?"

"You can carry it to the fields if a knackered back is what you want," Ernie chuckles.

"Ah, right, we're going in the Hog."

"*I'm* going in the Hog, but you my friend are going on this bad boy." He points, but whatever he's pointing at is obscured by a bale of hay. I clump towards him until it comes into view. A red quad bike. "Great little thing this. You'll have the wind in your hair, the sun on your face . . . probably a few flies down your throat," he laughs. "Only one problem though."

"What's that?"

"It's hard to start."

"Oh."

Ernie straddles it and talks me through what to do in what order. It seems fairly straightforward.

"You've got to be really nice to it up to this point, tell it it's lovely and that it's an important part of the team and suchlike, and then stroke its handlebars a few times, give it a pat on the belly, make it feel important. And then–"

The back of his fist skims my nose as he yanks the pull cord. He does it with such gusto that he's fully standing on the quad. My nose tingling and his face pink with the sudden rush of blood, we listen to the engine splutter into action then quickly peter out to lifeless silence. A cow moos as if mocking its failure.

"Bastard thing," Ernie says. He tries again, but with the same result, minus the moo. "Why don't you give it a go, Roy? You're a lot younger and stronger than me."

I get on the quad and set it up as he instructed. I look down at the pull cord, sizing it up like it's a boxing opponent.

"Yes! Well done!" Ernie says, with a fist of celebration. "Now give it a little throttle, keep it ticking over for a bit. Then drive it round to where we left the bags of grain."

We load the grain onto the back of the quad.

"Okay, so if you do the two fields closest to the farmhouse, I'll do the others. You'll see troughs in the middle of each of the fields. Stop the bike about five or six metres away, just like last night, then carry over the bag and fill up the troughs. Simple as that." He pats my back and points to the fields. "I'll get you back here when you're done. And remember the speed limit," he laughs. I give him the thumbs up and drive off towards my first field.

Once I've closed and secured the gate, I get back on the quad and drive towards the sheep which are running towards

224

me, their lambs tottering behind, every mouth bleating so loud that it's audible above the engine of the quad. It's a surreal moment, like I'm in a weird computer game, where the sheep are zombies but the lambs aren't – and I've got to mow down the sheep, save the lambs and get them to Ernie so he can give them a serum that ensures they never become hideous zombie sheep. And all before the timer runs out!

As I slow down, the sheep separate to let me through. Once I'm about six metres away from the troughs, I stop and get off the quad. The sheep surround me, bleating louder than ever and I can't help but laugh. Their faces look animated, like *Shaun the Sheep* from *Wallace & Gromit*. Leaving the engine ticking over, I carry the bag of grain to the troughs and laugh my way through filling them up, the grain sometimes landing on the heads or in the ears of over-zealous sheep. They're so fluffy and funny-looking, I reach down to pat one, but as soon as I make contact, it darts off away from the herd, albeit only for a few seconds. I feel relief in my muscles once the bag is empty. No wonder Ernie is buff for his age. I wonder how he'd look if he worked in an office. Like me.

I fold the bag and walk back to the quad, the sheep no longer interested in me. But just as I'm about to mount, I notice, in the far corner of the field, a sheep lying down. I jog over and, as I get closer, I see blue markings on its back. I'm conscious I have no sheepdog – and even if I did, I wouldn't know what to do with it – so I expect it to get up and run away. But it doesn't. There's half a lamb hanging out its rear end and another on the grass.

Using both hands, I pull gently on the lamb and it soon slips out without too much of a fuss. Covered in reddish-brown lining, its high-pitched bleats announce its arrival to the world. Remembering what Ernie did, I put my fingers in its mouth and clear it of mucus. The sheep gets up and backs off, its sac flopping around between its legs, bleating vociferously, made even louder by the engine of the quad cutting out.

"It's okay," I say, as if it knows English. "Everything's alright. Come and say hello." I help the lamb to its feet and then walk on my knees over to the other one. Its eyes are closed and short breaths make its stomach rise and fall quickly, like an over-exercised puppy. I stick my fingers in its mouth but there doesn't appear to be much mucus. I try again, going deeper, pinching my fingers together to try and find anything that could be restricting its breathing. The ewe is now licking the other twin, cleaning mucus and sinew off it. I wonder if its mother's tongue might help the struggling lamb.

"Come and see your other new arrival," I say, signaling for her to come over as if I'm a policeman on traffic duty, but as I go to pick it up, I see its stomach has stopped moving.

"No! No, no, no, no, no!"

Maybe I made it worse sticking my fingers down its throat. Maybe it would've been okay if I had just left it alone. I feel light-headed looking at its lifeless body.

Having had its fill of grain, a sheep from the troughs trots over, bleating aggressively. The new mother ignores it, continuing to clean its newborn. I stand up, walk towards it and shoo it away. It stops in its tracks, about four metres away, and continues bleating. The ewe, infatuated by her lamb, is right next to me. The decision is made only a split second before I wrestle her to the ground and tug with all my might at the blue wool on her back, tearing at it savagely like a demented animal.

Once I'm satisfied that there's no trace of blue, I stuff

the stained wool into the pocket of my waterproof and walk back to the dead lamb. The ewe rushes back to the other one and resumes cleaning. I kneel down and look at the lamb's lifeless face – eyes closed; mouth slightly open; tongue sticking out. Even though it only lasted a few seconds, I can still hear the ewe's screams as I tore at her coat, a loop in my brain playing it over and over. I pet the lamb, scratching it behind the ears, and my eyes become a little damp. The landscape is blurry as I scan for any witnesses and, at next blink, tears fall onto the lamb's smooth coat.

After nine attempts, I concede that the quad isn't going to start so I walk back, pick up the lamb and head for the woods. Four or five sheep follow, bleating disapproval, thinking I'm thieving one of their young for Sunday dinner. I scare them off with a snarl, jump the fence, and walk across the burn into the copse.

I dig as deep as I can without any tools. My muscles burn and fingers ache, but I keep working until I have a suitably-sized hole. Raindrops pitter on the leaves of the trees as I place the body in its grave.

"Rest in peace little one," I say, before replacing the soil and foliage. My eyes leak as the soil goes into the lamb's open mouth, clogging its now defunct airway. After everything is replaced, I check from various angles to see if anyone can tell there's been a disturbance. Once I'm satisfied, I walk back to the field and try the quad a few more times, without success. I lug the second bag of grain onto my shoulder and, with the sheep now much less interested in me, I head for the next field and all I can think about is Cooper.

*

"What happened to your nose?" Sandra asks as we sit down to lunch.

"Eh . . . I kinda punched myself in the face pulling the cord on the quad," I laugh.

"You really need to get rid of that thing, Ernest. It's getting less and less reliable as time goes on. It's a blooming good job Roy never got stuck somewhere much further away."

"I know, I know, I hear you," Ernie says, holding up his hands. "It's just that we've had it, what, 22, 23 years? It feels like part of the family, you know."

"I know, darling, but it's had its day, wouldn't you say?"

"Probably," Ernie shrugs. I'm pretty certain he's not going to get rid of it. He'll either get it fixed or it'll sit in a shed until it's a hunk of rust.

"Are you alright, Roy?" Sandra asks. "You look a bit pale."

"I'm fine, thanks, Sandra. Think I'm maybe just a little dehydrated. A nice big cup of tea will sort me out, especially the way you make it in that teapot."

"Coming up, my boy," she says. "You know, that teapot's been in the family for donkey's years and it's always made a perfect cup of tea."

"It's had its day if you ask me," Ernie says under his breath. Sandra either doesn't hear him or has chosen to ignore what he said.

I can't stop thinking about Cooper and Kristina. The Clayworths have a landline, but I've only been here a day. Asking to phone a mobile from their landline would be a bit inappropriate, or it would at least make me a little uncomfortable. Maybe there's a phone box in the village or a payphone at the pub, a few miles down the road. I could always investigate that. He'll be fine anyway. I would've heard if he was otherwise. Kristina would've looked the farm up online and called me. Yeah. He's a fighter. Everything will be okay.

After lunch, I go up to my room for a half hour's rest before heading back out onto the farm to feed the cattle and clean out the chicken coop. I lie on my bed and look at the pallid light through the Velux window. The rain has tamed to a drizzle. I glance out of the main window and tell myself that by the time I'm ready to get back to work, the sun will have nudged its way through and the day will once again be beautiful.

I pick up my phone. 1 new message. Kristina.

> Update on Cooper hes going to have t*some text missing*

No bars. I look at the time of message and it was a couple of hours ago. I lie back and throw my limbs out as if I'm doing a snow angel, and fall asleep.

I dream about the lamb. It digs its way out the grave, runs back to its mother and sibling and they bounce around in the field full of the joys of spring.

"Aw, isn't it cute?" Ernie says. "Yeah," I say, confused, looking at it. It winks at me. "Had you both worried for a minute there, didn't I?" it says. "Got to keep up the 100% record though, don't we, boys?"

I awake to a knock on my door. A little disorientated, I look out of the window to see the beginnings of a blue sky, my room notably brighter than before I fell asleep. I'd forgotten to set the alarm! Then I realise I hadn't actually intended on falling asleep. It's probably Sandra wondering where I am. Jeez, how long have I been asleep?

"Just a second." I kick a pair of dirty socks under the bed and then open the door.

"Hi, sorry I must've . . . Oh, hi."

"Hi," the girl says. She runs a hand through her long dark hair. "I'm Nora, Ernie and Sandra's niece."

"Nice to meet you," I say, holding out a hand. She shakes it, leans in and kisses my cheek. I feel something weird going on inside me. Weird but good.

"You're Roy, right?"

"Yeah. Yeah, sorry, I'm Roy," and I hold out my hand again, then blush at being so stupid, but before I can retract it, she shakes it again, laughs and kisses the other cheek.

"Sandra sent me up to see if you had any glasses or mugs and to ask if you're okay with spicy food 'cos she thought she'd make Rogan Josh for supper."

"Yeah, I'm fine with spicy food," I say, looking into her beautiful caramel eyes.

"I see a mug over there on your chest of drawers," she says, pointing over my shoulder. "Can I . . . come in?"

"Yeah . . . Yeah, of course you can."

We sit next to each other on the bed. She tells me about a local arts festival she ran last September and how she hopes to run it again this year. I look at her and nod, slightly dazed, not really taking it in, our faces coming closer and closer together until I'm in her personal bubble and know the light is green. Lips joined, we fall back onto the bed and run our hands through each other's hair. Life pulses through me. I pull her close so I can feel her heartbeat.

"There's something about this place," I say, as we part. "I feel totally different up here. It does something to me."

"It does something to you?" Nora giggles, resting her head on my shoulder. "Like what?"

"I don't know." I look through the Velux window at the

blue sky. "It's just strange to think this is the same country. I feel like I'm millions of miles away."

"I think you've had too much fresh air."

"Maybe that's it. Maybe it's the air."

"You know, I better take that mug down," Nora says. "Sandra will be wondering where I've got to."

"We've been . . . chatting," I say, tracing her curves with a finger. "You've been teaching me how to make the perfect refrigerator cake."

She smiles her alluring smile. "Yeah, Sandra told me you liked it."

"Loved it."

"It falls apart if you don't eat it or put it back in the fridge, you know."

"That's why Ernie and I polished it off," I laugh.

"Listen, how about we meet up in the pub tonight, once you and Uncle Ernie are done on the farm?"

"Yeah . . . yeah, that'd be great. Although I did say I'd watch *Match of the Day* with him."

"It's usually on quite late though, isn't it? Plus there's hardly ever a decent signal. Or he could always come with us. Okay, we wouldn't be alone, but I do love my Uncle Ernie. You should see him with a couple of pints in him. Honestly, what a laugh."

"Okay, cool. I'm sure we can work something out," I say, thinking I can use the pub's phone to find out more about Cooper. I check my phone before we head downstairs. 1 new message. Kristina.

```
Ok so things are now not looking
too*some text missing*
```

We can hear Ernie and Sandra laughing and flirting as we walk down the hall towards the kitchen. Nora and I share silent giggles.

"You took your time," Ernie says. "Fifteen minutes to retrieve one mug."

"I was giving him my refrigerator cake recipe."

"What? But I thought that was a family secret?" Ernie says, turning serious.

"Aw, don't worry, I didn't give him the *exact* recipe," Nora says with a wink. Ernie holds out his pinky for pinky promise. Nora interlocks it with hers and watches his serious face break into a big, goofy grin.

"Okay, so is everyone good to go?" Sandra says, lifting her waterproof off the coat stand. "Nora and I are going to lunge the horses then muck out the stables while you two feed the cattle, and if we've got time before starting the supper, we'll do a quick check of the nearby fields as well." She lifts my waterproof next and throws it over. A clump of blue wool falls from the pocket and lands on the tiles. "So, come on, the sooner we get started, the sooner we'll be done and we can all sit down to a lovely meal and a great big glass of wine."

"Sounds good to me," Nora says.

I stand on the wool and put on my waterproof.

"Ernest." Sandra throws him his. "Come on, let's go. Wellies on, everyone."

"Yes, boss, anything you say, boss," Ernie laughs. He looks at me. "Actually, she *is* the boss."

"You wouldn't have it any other way, would you, Uncle Ernie?" Nora says, patting him on the shoulder.

"Do you want the real answer or the answer I've been trained to give?" he jokes.

Sandra walks out of the door, followed by Ernie and then Nora. When Nora realises I'm not following her, she turns back with a smile. She's the prettiest girl I've ever seen.

"Aren't you coming, Roy?"

Thanks in Advance

"Yes, sir, what can I get you?"

"Pint of lager, please."

The barman lifts a pint glass from below the bar, twirls it on his palm and places the nozzle of the juice gun into it. Lemonade fizzes out as he looks out of the window, whistling.

"Excuse me," I say. "It was a pint of lager I asked for."

"Was it? I could've sworn you said a lager shandy. Sorry about that, sir. A pint of lager, you say?"

"Yeah, please."

"No problem, coming up."

He lifts another pint glass, twirls it on his palm and raises it to the nozzle of the lager tap. The golden liquid pours into the glass. I swallow, but there's nothing to go down my throat, I'm so parched. I look out the window as a white limousine passes with its windows down, girls hanging out wearing pink cowboy hats, waving at random strangers. When I look back, the barman is topping up the lager with lemonade.

"I should've done this the other way round, eh?" he says. "It would've been easier to put the lemonade in first, I think."

"No, no, stop! I didn't ask for a shandy! It's a pint of lager I want. No lemonade!"

"Well, why didn't you ask for that in the first place? And will you please calm down. This is a respectable public house, you know."

"Sorry . . . sorry . . . but that is what I asked for."

"Pint of lager?" The barman says.

"Yes. A pint of lager. Please"

"Coming up."

He lifts another pint glass, twirls it on his palm and picks up the juice gun. I say nothing and watch him make a lager shandy.

"There we are, sir." He places it on the bar with a smile. "One pint of lager. That's £3.50 please."

F R I D A Y

I wake up groggy and confused. Teri is fast asleep, mouth open with a dried trail of drool on her left cheek. Brandy looks up at me with her big black eyes, whimpering.

"Needing out for a pee, pal?" She stretches and yawns, her pink tongue unfathomably long, as if it belongs to a cartoon greyhound. I heave myself up and sit on the edge of the bed for a while, rubbing my face; ruffling my hair; scratching the blotchy skin on my belly.

"Okay, girl, let's go."

I groan getting to my feet and then plod through to the kitchen, Brandy weaving around me, looking up expectantly. I let her out to the back garden, leave the door open and walk back to the bedroom. Teri winces when I switch on the big light.

"We need to get a lower wattage bulb for that bloody thing," she snaps, pulling the duvet up over her head.

After the cumbersome job of changing my boxers and putting on a clean pair of socks, I open my side of our mirrored wardrobe and sigh at my lack of options. I pull on a pair of red jeans and a black shirt. Black's best for sweat rings. When I close the door, I grimace at my reflection.

"Teri, have you been using different washing powder or something? This shirt feels like it's shrunk."

"You just need to stop eating crap, Mel. And exercise more. It's not rocket science," she shouts through the duvet.

I place my hands on my gut and shrug at my reflection. "You're one to talk," I mutter under my breath.

"What was that?"

"Nothing. Just talking to myself."

I switch off the big light and stand over the bed. When she emerges, I kiss her forehead.

"Aw, you still love me even though I'm a cranky-pants." I look at my watch to see if I've got a couple of minutes to sit down and stroke her hair.

"Christ, is that the time? Look, can you feed the dog, sweetheart? I've got to get out of here!"

"Okay, honey, will do. Have a good day."

I glance in the little mirror in the hall and quickly run my hands through my hair, which needs cut. Brandy pads in from the kitchen and looks up, knowing I'm leaving.

"It's alright, pal, Mummy's here all day today, remember? She'll give you your breakfast in a minute. Daddy's got to go, but I'll be back later and we can play then, okay?" I kneel down, kiss her long snout and stroke her back. When I lever myself up, I have to grip the handle of the cupboard. I turn my back on her, lift my jacket off its hook and open the front door. I can't stand seeing her dipped head and questioning, disappointed eyes.

"Bye, honey!" I shout. I hear a response but can't make it out. When I don't see the car in its usual spot, I remember the street was packed last night when we came back from the pictures and I had to park over in Wilson Terrace.

"Shit!" I break into a jog. A couple of high school kids

on the other side of the road point and laugh. Once I reach the car, I get in, start the engine and roll down the window. I wait for the dizziness to settle and, panting, I pull off, blue smoke billowing down the street behind me.

Crunching leftover boiled sweets from the pictures, I think about The Huddleston Report. The more I think about it, the faster I drive, Gus's voice in my head criticising my *lack of attention to detail in certain areas*, my *tendency for overlong sentences*, my *occasional inability to think outside the box, but having said that I can see you are actually capable of it, Brock.*

"Morning, Terry," I gasp, pushing my damp fringe out of my eyes.

"Morning, Mel," he replies, buzzing me in. "Running a little late today, are we?"

I bound up two flights of stairs and into the office. Sweat drips onto my keyboard as I quickly log in. I look at the clock and then my watch.

"30 seconds!" I collapse onto my chair.

"Christ, you like cutting it fine, don't you?" Clarence laughs, feet on his desk, sipping coffee from his GOD OF MY OWN WORLD mug.

"On time is on time, Clarence."

I open my bottom drawer and lift out a can of deodorant and a kitchen roll. Tasting salt, I dab myself dry, which takes up what's left of the roll as I need to cover most areas more than once.

"How did you get on with The Huddleston Report?" Marco asks, pushing back the bridge of his glasses with his forefinger, even though they hadn't slipped. "Gus said anything about it yet?"

"Not yet," I say, trying to regulate my breathing and stop

my heart from wanting to jump out my chest. "But I'm guessing I'll be the first to know."

"Oh, you can bank on that, Melvin," Clarence says. "You can *definitely* bank on that."

From my slumped, exhausted state, I imagine leaping up, ninja-style, and fly-kicking Clarence in the chest, so he falls back in his chair, breaks his back and scalds his priggish face with boiling hot coffee.

"I'd be happy to let you know what he says once I hear, Clarence. It's important we share these things."

"Really? Oh, come on, you're taking the piss, right?"

"No, not at all. I think it's important that, as a group, we help each other develop an understanding of the expectations of our manager."

I spray deodorant around my workspace, hoping that some of it will go in Clarence's coffee or at least catch the back of his throat. "If anyone's looking for me, I'm just going to the vending machines, okay?"

When I return, stocked up, crunching a mouthful of crisps, Gus is in the office.

"Ah, there you are, Brock. I was just telling Fletcher and Baird that head office has informed me that there's a lot of stuff coming our way. So look lively and be alert. I'll be looking for good things from you lot."

"Yes, boss," I say.

"Feeling peckish again, are we, Brock? May I be so bold as to suggest that it might be a good idea to start the day with healthy, slow release foods. Porridge, for example. Diet can have a significant impact on productivity, you know, and I need you . . . all of you . . ." – he points at us in an arc – "to be as productive . . . as . . . possible."

" . . ."

"You have porridge every morning, don't you, Baird?"

"Without fail, Mr Hilton."

"Me too," Clarence pipes up. "Well, alternated with Shredded Wheat."

"Very good, Fletcher. Much better than . . ." He snatches one of my packets. "Mini Cheddars, wouldn't you say, Brock?"

"Yes, sir. I'll look into it."

"Glad to hear it. Now, let's get a move on, shall we? Time is money."

Inwardly groaning, I place some of my stash next to my keyboard and the rest in my bottom drawer. When the door closes and the clip-clop of Gus's shiny black shoes fades, I look over to Clarence.

"What?"

"You're such a fucking brown-nose" I shake my head.

He leans over, hands cupped round his mouth. "Still nothing on The Huddleston Report," he whispers.

The morning drags, but I get the office to myself in the afternoon as Clarence and Marco have to attend a conference somewhere across town. Grazing on nuts and chocolate, I get loads done and before long, it's time to log off and head home. I shut down all programs except my email, and look at the clock.

"20 seconds to go." Finger poised, I hover over the red X and watch the second hand tick towards freedom. And then *ding*.

From: Gus Hilton
To: Melvin Brock
Date: 31 January 2014, 04.59PM
Subject: Re: The Huddleston Report

A couple of things, Brock:

1) There are a few touch-ups required on The Huddleston Report but overall what you've produced is useful. I'll send you an email on Monday with suggested edits, but for future reference I'd recommend using more appropriate adjectives. And please learn the function of a semi-colon.

2) Another job has just come in – The McCusker Report – but I'm unable to deal with it this weekend due to the golf. This means I'll have to put my trust in you to take things forward. It also means you'll have to work tomorrow and probably Sunday too. I've left the keys with Terry at security. He knows you'll be picking them up when you leave the office today. The files and your instructions have been posted on the B Drive under 'McCusker'. Just to note, there will be no extra payment for your time for this as it falls under "Other duties and responsibilities pertinent to the post" in your job description. If you have any questions, you can email me, but don't expect an instant reply.

I know this may be inconvenient, especially if you have plans this weekend, but please remember that jobs like this are difficult to come across and the management team is putting their faith in you to deliver. If you do a good job, it may enhance promotion opportunities, although that's not something I can guarantee.

3) Finally, your attire. Although your engagements with clients and the public are minimal, ill-fitting red jeans are not appropriate for this company. I'd also recommend acquiring a shirt you can tuck in which actually stays tucked in. Perhaps you could consult Fletcher and/or Baird as they are always impeccably dressed. There'd be no harm in cutting your hair either, or at least brushing it out of your eyes, especially for videoconferencing/Skype activities.

Thanks in advance,

Gus.

S A T U R D A Y

"I can't believe you've got to go to work today! Can't you just phone in sick or something? Tell them there's been a family crisis, or . . . or a bereavement. No-one questions a bereavement."

"Teri, I can't. You know I can't."

"But I want to go up the coast with Brandy, Mel . . . and throw stones in the water . . . and then go to that chip shop we went to last time, remember? How good were those chips?"

I sit up and stare at the carpet, willing myself to get

moving. My head's trying to make sense of my recurring lager shandy dream – and why I thought drinking seven cans of lager last night was a good idea (it was Friday night!) As I think about the chips, a string of saliva leaks from my mouth onto my thigh. I lick my lips and close my mouth.

"Remember how golden they were on the outside," Teri continues. "And fluffy on the inside."

"Yeah," I say, wiping my slavers off my thigh with the blade of my hand.

"Honestly, Mel, you need to start looking for another job, I've had it with that place. You're always knackered when you come home and those guys you work with – fucking Marky and Cuthbert or whatever – sound like complete twats. And as for Gus, does he really think it's okay to spring shit like this on you at the last minute? I mean, *really*?"

"It's an opportunity, Teri," I say, pulling on a clean pair of socks, grimacing at my flaky feet. "Jeezo, my mouth's like cotton."

"An opportunity? An opportunity for what?" She turns her back on me, rolling herself in the duvet like a pig in a blanket. Brandy pads over and rests her snout on my leg.

"Well, who knows, if I make a good job of this McCusker Report, it could lead to a promotion . . . then we could maybe afford a decent holiday this year."

" . . . "

"Cos I was thinking, right . . . Clarence and Marco were dying to see me shot down in flames for The Huddleston Report, but Gus has said that there are only minor touch-ups needed. So maybe he's given me the McCusker Report because he knows I'll do a good job – and if I do, it'll put me ahead of those two tossers in the promotion race."

" . . . "

I force myself up and plod round the bed, Brandy in tow.

"Come on, girl, let's get us some breakfast."

I log in with four minutes to spare and head to the vending machine. Munching Maltesers, I click into the B Drive, open the McCusker file and read the instructions. My jaw slows to a halt. The malty, chocolatey mush slips down my throat of its own accord.

"Fuck me."

I eat a packet of prawn cocktail crisps really quickly, as if searching for a magical crisp that will sort my head out. I scrunch the packet and lean back in my chair sipping a can of Diet Coke. I remind myself that this is an opportunity. If I nail it, I could start earning some real money. I guzzle the Diet Coke, slam dunk the can in the bin, rub my hands together and get started.

It's intense, exhausting stuff. Some of the people I phone aren't happy being disturbed on a Saturday morning, but I manage to get all the information I need. About three quarters of the way through the morning, my screen freezes and tingles of dread shoot up my spine. Thankfully, it's just the machine slowing down because I've got so many programs running at the same time. Save save save. I shut a few down, rub my face and keep going.

When lunchtime comes, I'm pleased with the progress I've made, so I head out to the burger van over the road. I return with a quarter pounder and a chicken burger and go online to have a look at the football fixtures. I open a new window, log into Paddy Power and put on a long line accumulator. Some of my choices are based on what I know about the team or league but others are just random, like Torquay, York City and Ayr United. I put on a couple of Sunday games too, Watford to beat Brighton & Hove Albion and Nottingham Forest to beat Yeovil Town. I nearly leave it at that, until I see Chelsea is away to Man City on Monday night. I put down Chelsea to win and bet £25. If all 12 teams come in, I win £189,308.

"Waste of £25," I say, shaking my head. My mobile rings.

"Hi, honey, how you doing?"

"Shite, that's how I'm doing," Teri says. "Brandy has just cut her paw on a bottle some arsehole has smashed on the path next to the park. I had her on the extender lead and was looking at my phone. Then I heard her yelp."

"Aw, you're joking!" I pace about, ruffling my hair.

"I wish I *was* joking. I'm taking her up to the vet's just now. Thing is, I've only got a couple of quid on me. What am I going to do if it costs a fortune?"

"Jeez, how bad is it? My poor little pal!"

"Well, it's bleeding and she's probably got shards in her pads. I'm trying to stop her from licking it in case she ends up hurting her tongue as well."

I can hear her whimpering in the background.

"What an arsehole!"

"What?"

"The guy who smashed the bottle. Fucking arsehole!"

"I know, I'm raging about it too."

"Listen, don't worry about money." I say, sitting down. "Just make sure she gets fixed up okay. The vet's a decent sort, isn't she? Tell her she can phone me and we can do a bank transfer, or I can post cash through her door on my way home or something."

"Right, okay, hopefully that'll be fine . . . Okay, I'd better get going. I'll let you know how I get on."

"Okay, honey. Give Brandy a kiss for me."

"Will do. Speak to you later. Love you."

"Love you too, hon."

As soon as I hang up, my desk phone rings.

"Hello?"

"Brock, it's me. How's the McCusker Report coming along?"

"Fine, sir." I sit up in my chair as if he's standing behind me. "So far, so good. Making decent progress."

"Not too challenging for you, then? A walk in the park, is it?"

"Well, not quite, sir." I point my conference-cam to the ceiling and tuck my red-jeaned legs under my desk. "There's a lot to it, but I'm chipping away. How are things on the golf course?"

"Never mind that, Brock," Gus snaps. "Now listen here and listen good. If you *ever* use a company computer for gambling again, I will personally boot your fat arse out the door before you can say peanut M&Ms. Do I make myself clear?"

"Yes, sir."

"How clear, Brock? How clear?"

"Crystal, sir."

"Good. Now get back to work. I'm expecting good things from you. Don't let me down."

I hear the crack of a driver hitting a ball.

"Sir?"

"Yes?"

" . . . "

" . . . "

"Can you see me?"

"I'm on a fucking golf course, Brock!"

"Sorry, sir, I–"

"You think I've hidden a camera in the office, don't you? For fuck's sake, I'm not that untrusting, Brock, and I resent the accusation."

"Sorry, sir, I wasn't accusing you–"

"I'm the CEO of the company, Brock. Even remotely, I can check in to see what activity there's been. Now I suggest you take your mind off what *I'm* doing and get back to The McCusker Report, don't you agree?"

"Yes, sir." I move my legs out from underneath the desk.

"Good. I'll look forward to seeing your work on Monday morning. Goodbye."

"Bye, sir," but the line is dead.

I take a Snickers out of my drawer, open The McCusker Report and get back to work. An hour later, Teri phones. The shards of glass have been picked out of Brandy's paw and it's been bandaged up, but she does have to wear a cone while it heals. The vet understood Teri's circumstances and agreed that the fee of £58 could be posted later on. Based on a stuttering start to the afternoon session on The McCusker Report, and even though I can tell Teri wants to chat for a bit, I cut the conversation short and get back to work.

Time passes quickly and I start to panic about the lack of progress I've made. One part of the report is really challenging and I spend over two hours dealing with it. Knackered and frustrated, I look at the clock – 4.31pm – and decide I need a break. I text Teri to let her know I'm going to be late and saunter to the internet café down the road.

Sipping a hazelnut macchiato, I use one of the café's computers to check my coupon. My disbelief swells as team after team comes in. Eight out of nine. York City are winning 2-1 against Fleetwood, but it's only the latest. I bring up the live feed and wait, scalp perspiring as I shift around in my seat, tapping out-of-time rhythms onto the table.

Result.

"Yes! Yes!" Face hot with glee, I punch towards the floor. Anyone looking would think there was something wrong with me. "Come on, three to go," I say under my breath, knowing I can't get too excited. I down the remainder of my coffee and head back to the office. I do another couple of hours on The McCusker Report and then head home via the vet's, off-license and kebab shop, knackered.

SUNDAY

"Brandy, you're not allowed up here, remember."

"Oh, just let her, Mel, the poor soul's been in the wars," Teri says, standing over the bed.

"Okay, but don't get used to it, creep." I stroke her snout. Her pathetic expression says *get this bloody lampshade off me.* "You'll be better soon, pal, don't you worry."

"You getting up then?" Teri says.

"Suppose I'll have to, yeah . . . Jeezo, that bloody dream!"

"What dream? What are you on about?"

"I keep dreaming that I'm in a pub asking for a pint of lager, but the barman pours me a shandy. I tell him no, not a shandy, just a pint of lager – and then he pours me another shandy! This goes on and on until we're nearly fighting. Last night, he was raging at me for wasting his stock, finger in my face demanding that I'm clear about what I want. So I ask for a pint of lager. And he pours me another shandy!"

"Well, why don't you order a shandy and see if you end up with a pint of lager," Teri says, nonchalantly, pulling a jumper over her head.

"I hadn't thought of that. But it's a dream. I can't just change what I'm dreaming, can I? If I could, I'd have him pouring lager instead of shandy."

249

"Just saying."

" . . . "

" . . . "

"How come you're up anyway?"

"I knew you'd forget! I need the car today, remember. I'm dropping you off at the office and then taking Mum to look at new bathrooms."

"Oh yeah, rings a bell. Sorry, all I can think about is this bloody McCusker Report."

"It's okay, honey, but remember you'll need to get the bus back tonight, and they're only once an hour on a Sunday."

"Yeah, okay," I yawn.

"Right, come on, then, time to get up. Tell him, Brandy."

Seeing the office for the seventh day in a row is soul-destroying, especially since I know I'll be seeing it for another five before I get a break. But at least Clarence and Marco aren't here. I log in and head to the vending machine for supplies. When I return, chomping a Topic, I open The McCusker Report, review what I've done and cringe at how much I've still to do, the only silver lining being that the most complex section has been dealt with.

I work for about an hour and a half then have to stop as my eyes are stinging. I blame the screen, but lack of sleep and the five bottles of pear cider I had last night won't have helped. I plod around the office, blinking and stretching, making noises. On Marco's desk there's a framed photograph of him topless, standing next to some other guy who's also topless. They've got football shirts in their hands, one red and one white. I don't recognize the player as anyone famous. Both have big cheesy grins and six-packs, but Marco's muscle definition is more impressive, although his arms are smaller.

I walk across to Clarence's desk. Between his desk tidy and GOD OF MY OWN WORLD mug, there's a photograph of him and his wife at a Halloween party dressed as Posh and Becks. I don't know what's scarier, them choosing Posh and Becks or that they actually pull it off quite well. I look closer at his wife. How did he manage to bag her? It surely can't be his chat. I try to open his top drawer but it's locked. They're all locked. This is probably a good thing, I decide.

Regularly munching my stash, I manage to stay focused on the report and get plenty done. At 4.42, I head to the café, order a vanilla latte and sit down at one of the computers.

"Come on Watford, come on Forrest."

I click into the results page.

"Yeeeeeeees!" I jump up off my seat and punch the air. "Fucking yeeeeeees!"

Apart from the parp of trumpets from the stereo, the café falls silent.

"Sorry. I'm really sorry." I turn to make eye contact with everyone. "Sorry. Sorry. Sorry. Just got some good news there. Sorry. Sorry."

"Vanilla latte?" The waitress says.

"Yes, thank you. Thank you very much." I hand her a substantial tip. I sip the latte, staring blankly at the screen, thinking about what I'd spend the money on if Chelsea does the business tomorrow night. Someone's got to beat Man City at home. Law of averages. "Come on, Chelsea. Come-on-come-on-come-on," I mutter to myself.

I run my hands down my jeans, cutting little white lines into the red. I finish my coffee, buy a prawn baguette and head back to the office. I sit in my office chair and eat the baguette, crumbs snowing onto my shirt like dandruff. I open The McCusker Report, but I'm distracted. I can't help thinking of Man City's outstanding home form, scoring 104 goals this season so far. I flit from taking it as a dead cert to surmising that such exceptional home form can't last forever. I look at the screen, The McCusker Report staring back at me, incomplete. If Chelsea win I could chuck it. I wouldn't need to work for at least three years, maybe five. It'd be great to get away from Clarence and Marco. Gus too. I could hire a personal trainer. Teri and I could go on a lavish holiday.

At 9.47, bleary-eyed and listless, I save The McCusker Report in the B Drive's password-protected folder, adding FINAL to the title. I email Gus with the password and shut down my computer, resisting the temptation to tell him to shove his job up his arse. I carefully prise myself out my chair. The sweat between my bum cheeks makes them squelch and my thighs feel like they're going to spasm, but don't. I dust any remaining crumb dandruff off my shirt and watch it fall to the floor. It lands next to an escaped prawn. After carefully shaking out my legs, I crouch down and pick it up. One of the compartments of Clarence's desk tidy is packed tight with pens. I pull them out, drop in the prawn and replace the pens exactly where they were.

When I get off the bus, I cross the park to get home. As I walk towards the road at the other side, I see a group of teenagers standing at a hedge, drinking. On the path and in the gutter are empty cans and bottles, some smashed. A tall, thin, but fairly muscular guy who looks like he fancies himself as a rapper is pissing into the opposite gutter. He looks at me as I approach, but keeps going, his stream dancing in the air to the amusement of the girls of the group.

"Got a light, mate?" he shouts, tucking his snake into his jeans, which look like they're about to fall off his arse.

"No."

"Fuck's sake, he's a big unit," says one of the guys by the hedge.

"Yeah, definitely not built for speed," says another.

I walk past them, making no eye contact. They titter and snort.

"Hiya, gorgeous," laughs one of the girls.

I keep going, pretending I'm unaffected, until they're out of earshot.

I walk along a couple of towpaths and turn into Wilson Terrace. About 200 yards away, walking towards the towpath at the other end of the terrace, is the tall rapper guy, alone, swigging from a bottle of wine. He's got big headphones on and is throwing his hands about like he's Dr Dre or Snoop Doggy-Dogg. I start to jog, instantly feeling the strain on my knees. As I get closer, I hear how loud his music is. He throws back his head, guzzles what's left and hurls the bottle into the gutter.

I get speed from somewhere, and a moment of perfect clarity, then we're on the ground and my hand is squeezing his windpipe. His face advances from red to purple as he struggles for breath. "Open your fucking mouth, but if you scream, I swear I'll kill you." I say, releasing the pressure. "Now eat this." I force the neck of the broken bottle into his mouth. "Eat. Eat!" Blood splurges from his lips like runny egg yolk. I release my grip. He spits out pieces of glass, gasping for breath. I roll him onto his front and pull off his hoodie and t-shirt. "Get off me you fat fucker," he splutters. I drag him onto his bed of glass, stand up and grind him into it with my foot like I'm using a towel to mop something up from the kitchen floor.

When I get home, I have a shower and think about Chelsea. Teri is asleep and Brandy is stretched out on my side of the bed. I stand next to her, naked. She looks up with forgiving eyes.

"Hello, girl," I say, stroking her snout. "You feeling better today?"

She licks my hand and raises her damaged paw, not for me to examine, but as an invite to rub her belly.

"Aw, who's a pretty girl, eh?"

I pull on a pair of boxer shorts, get into bed and push Brandy over a bit. Teri stirs, but doesn't wake up. I droop my arm over my best pal and look into Teri's closed eyes, wondering how I'm going to tell her. *If* I'm going to tell her. I stroke Brandy's belly until I drift off to sleep.

"Yes, sir, what can I get you?"

"Pint of lager, please."

The Traitor's Treble

"You'll be missing the game today then, Jack?"

"Christ, step aside Sherlock Holmes," I say, a bit of burger jumping out the side of my mouth. "I know I like my team, but I wasn't going to miss big Kev's 50th barbecue."

The combination of sunlight, starchy food and strong cider has already begun to take its effect. I'm in that content, mellow zone where I'm fed but not bloated, drunk but not legless and chatty whilst still making sense.

But it's only 4 o' clock.

And even though I don't want to eat until it hurts, or wake up tomorrow with a hangover, I know it's probably going to happen. Kev's wife, Judy, has spent a fortune on food and booze. Burgers, sausages, chicken and kebabs sizzle on the barbecue, the double fridge in the garage is full of beer, cider and wine, and there's a huge bowl of punch, deep red in colour, on a table alongside salad, sauces and relishes, and three kingsize bags of pink marshmallows.

To stop now would be downright rude.

"Where are you sitting in the table at the moment anyway?" Reilly asks. He's not actually bothered, he's just making idle chit-chat. To entertain myself, I consider telling him we're top, but decide against it, realising that he wouldn't know one way or the other so I'd really just be teasing myself. And that's not entertaining.

"Seventh, man."

"Aw, that's not bad, and there's everything to play for at this stage of the season, isn't there?" he says, sounding like he knows what he's talking about. I tip back my can and swallow the dregs.

"Yip. Sure is."

"You fancy another of those . . . what are they called . . ." – he takes the empty can from me – "Scrumpy Jack's? I'm going to the fridge."

"Well, if you're going, yeah, thanks, man."

I finish my burger and pick up another roll.

"Did I hear him trying to talk about football?" says Ellie, big Kev's daughter, turning sausages with her tongs.

"Yeah," I laugh.

"Honestly, he does my head in. Like, why does he think he has to talk about it when he's clearly not interested?"

> Ellie was amazing. A—may—zing.
> Never had anything like it my life.
> Think about it every time I look at
> her. Never thought I'd ever experience
> anything as good ever again. Until
> the second time. If I'd died during
> it, I'd have died happy. That thing
> she did. Pressed a button that hadn't
> been pressed before. Didn't even know
> such a button existed.

"Stick a couple of sausages on there, will you, Elles?" I say, holding out my roll.

> Could take her right now. Tear off
> that apron. Take the bun out her hair.
> Do it behind the king-size bags of
> marshmallows. Hope no-one notices
> 'cos they're too busy filling their faces with
> dead animals and alcohol.

257

She lifts one sausage at a time on to my roll. "You should try my mum's homemade spicy relish, it's totally amazing," she says.

A—may—zing

"There's, like, just the right amount of heat in it. Enough to make you go oooooh, but not enough to leave your mouth on fire."

I replay the cute face she pulled when she said oooooh.

Oooooh

Oooooh

"Where is your dad, anyway?" I say, spooning the relish onto my sausages. "I've hardly seen him since I arrived."

"Up there with Reilly, heading this way" she says, pointing over my shoulder with her meat-smeared tongs. I turn to see them coming down the patio steps to the garden and towards us.

"Jack, my man," Kev slurs. "I was just telling Reilly here that he talks out his arse 92% of the time. That leaves only 8% sense. Did you know that?"

"What, that Reilly talks out his arse or that 92 plus eight is a hundred?"

Reilly laughs along. Ellie and I share a glance.

"Talking about the beautiful game again, Reilly?" I say. "You know, I reckon you talk about football more than any of us – and you're the only one who isn't into it. We can talk about other things, man."

"The *beautiful* game?" he says, passing me my can.

"Beautiful!" Kev punches the air and then rests it on Reilly's shoulder. "More beautiful than your wife, Reilly."

"Dad!" Ellie says.

"Are you telling me that Arbroath football club is a more beautiful thing than my Sandie?" Reilly says. Ellie turns round to hide her laugh, but mine and Kev's just blurt out.

Stone-faced, Reilly's eyes dart between me, Kev and the back of Ellie's head.

"You know, I think you're probably right," he says.

Kev spits out a mouthful of lager. Ellie turns back, wide-mouthed. "You can't say that about your wife!"

"You can't say that about Arbroath," I laugh.

"I fuckin' love you guys," Kev says, holding up his can. We clunk them together and take big swigs.

"Right, Reilly, let's talk about something other than football. Your shout," I say through a mouthful of sausage and doughy mush.

We get talking about reality TV and how it's seen better days. Ellie serves up some venison burgers and Kev manages to stagger his way to the fridge for more booze. He returns with his arm around his other daughter, Skye.

"Ellie, Skye's going to do the marshmallows, so clean all that meat off the barbie, will you? . . . Or hang on, maybe we could just have them kinda meaty. D'you fancy a venison marshmallow, Jack? There's venison marshmallows everyone!"

"Oh my God, how much has he had to drink?" Skye asks me.

Mind blowing. Better than
the first time with Ellie but not as good
as the second. But the noises she made. I
never thought
I could make anyone make noises like that.
And nearly half my age too. I felt like George
Clooney. Full head of hair. Toned.
Silver Fox. But it was definitely just me.
I did that. Me.

"It's nothing to do with me," I say, innocently. "I've only seen him have a couple."

"He's only had, like, six or something," Ellie says.

"Venison marshmallows! I wonder what they actually taste like, eh? You up for trying one, Reilly? Come on, it'll be mental. *We'll* be mental. Does anyone know the Arbroath score?"

"You're a lightweight, Dad," Skye says.

Could place a melted marshmallow
on her belly button and lick out
the pink goo. Wonder what kind
of noise she'd make. If it'd
get her going. If it'd be a way in for
a second time. Wonder if she'd find
that button, like Ellie did.

"How are you anyway, Jack? Not seen you for a while."

"Fine, darling," I say, cringing at how sleazy 'darling' sounds with a slight slur. "How's yourself? Still doing all that pom-pom stuff?"

"Yeah, like a little girl at, like, primary school or something," Kev says over his shoulder, staggering off to speak to his cousins and their kids, one of which is blowing bubbles.

"You mean cheerleading," Skye laughs.

Could ask her to practice one of her routines for me.
She could cast her clothes bit by bit
until all that's left are the
pom-poms. Just the
pom-poms.
Nothing
else.

"Yeah, well you do use pom-poms, don't you?"

"You're funny," she says, running her hands through her hair.

"You need to work on your sense of humour if you think this clown's funny," Reilly says. "Although the football team he supports is a joke."

"Will you shut up about football, Reilly," I say, loudly, but still jokingly. "We all know you're desperate to fit in, man, but just give it up, nobody likes you, alright?"

"God, why are you all so bloody horrible to each other?" Ellie says.

"Well, apart from Ellie, she thinks you're alright."

Reilly laughs along and doesn't retort. I'm not sure if it's because he can't think of a comeback line or if he's worried that Ellie might think we genuinely do dislike each other.

"Another beer, Reilly, man? What about you, Skye? You wanting another one of those . . . what is that?"

She downs what's in her glass and hands me it. "Gin and tonic," she says, licking her lips.

Could tickle me all over with the pom-poms.

Get me all tingly.

I walk up the garden burping and nearly trip on the first step leading up to the patio. Folk I don't know look over and laugh. A guy drinking something blue asks me if I'm alright and I say I'm fine, even though it's clear I am. I wonder what he'd have done if I said no and asked him to phone an ambulance, then I wonder why I'm wondering and burp a meaty, cidery burp.

I get chatting to Swannie in the kitchen, an old pal who came to Arbroath games with me and Kev until he had to start working weekends.

"Gutted I'm missing the game, Swannie, man. What can you do though, eh?"

"Tell me about it, 'cos I was going to go as I'm off this weekend – obviously!" he says, pointing at himself with two thumbs. "But it makes sense to have this in the afternoon for the family and the kids and all that. Plus you can't really have a barbecue at night, can you?"

"I know, man, you're right. I bet you'll have a line on though, won't you?"

"Of course. Montrose to win, Forfar to win and us to lose to Brechin. Traitor's Treble, man," he grins.

"You are joking! Same here! Put it there, man!" I hold out my hand. He shakes it hard then reaches into his pocket for his mobile phone.

"And it's up at the moment. 1-0 to Montrose, 2-0 to Forfar and we're getting beat 2-1 with about 20 minutes plus stoppages to go."

"Quality, man! Well, it's no quality we're getting beat, but The Traitor's Treble coming in takes the sting out it, eh?"

"There's nothing sore about being £300 up," Swannie says. "C'mon the Gable Endies!"

"Easy, man, eaaaasy! That's taking it too far," I laugh. "Hey, Kev!" I shout out to the garden. "We're 2-1 down."

"Fuck me," he shouts back, instantly cupping his hands over his mouth whilst looking down at the kids.

Swannie and I laugh. "How much you due to win?" he asks.

"Not as much as you, but it'll still be a decent little wager. 120 quid."

We get chatting about this season's squad, who's done well, who's underperformed, who should get kept for next season, best goal so far and all that, and then Ellie bursts in.

"What's going on, Jack?"

"What do you mean, what's going on?"

"Where are Reilly and Skye's drinks? They've been waiting ages." I'm waiting for her face to crack into a smile. "And how come you never offered me one, eh? I was standing right next to you, cleaning the rack for the marshmallows. Am I, like, invisible or something?"

> Imagine her in a devil's costume,
> horns on head, poker in hand.
> Red high heels
> Angry at me for not asking her
> if she wanted a drink.
> Ties me up, drips candle wax
> over me

"Sorry, hen. What you on? Voddie?"

"Yeah, but I'm here now, so what does it matter?" She slams glasses down onto the worktop and tips vodka and gin into them.

"Look, I said I was sorry, I didn't mean to not include you. I just . . . just–"

"Just what, Jack?" She throws the tonic water onto one of the shelves of the fridge and slams the door. I chuckle at the lack of noise. A fridge door isn't the best choice of door to slam to show anger.

"Nothing, nothing," I say, hands up, as if she's pointing a pistol at me.

> Like a cowgirl who's strolled
> into town to show me who's
> boss, wearing just boots,
> denim shorts and a Stetson

"Whatever. You can get Reilly's drink." She storms outside. I watch her walk across the patio, all smiles at her Auntie Gayle and Uncle Graeme.

"Amazing."

264

"Amazing?" says Swannie.

"Eh . . ."

"Fuckin' mentalist if you ask me," he chuckles, lifting a bottle to his mouth.

I open the fridge and quickly pick out a beer for Reilly and a cider for myself. "I better get going, Swannie. I'll catch up with you later, man."

"No bother, Jack, I'll let you know the final scores."

"Cheers, man," I say over my shoulder, walking out the door.

I spend the next 20 minutes with Skye, Ellie and Reilly. We eat gooey marshmallows of the non-venison kind and talk about Les Dennis and how Amanda Holden cheated on him with Neil Morrissey. And maybe I'm just imagining it, but the more Reilly drinks, the more his eyes look that lustful, sleazy way towards Ellie and Skye.

"Jack!" Swannie shouts, jumping off the patio steps onto the grass. "Coupon's up, man!"

We do a silly dance, miss each other with high fives and share an awkward bear hug because he's so tall. Heads turn at our celebration, but we don't care. The Traitor's Treble is up.

I get pissed. Ellie berates me for putting us on to lose and our archrivals to win, but I try to explain that it numbs the pain. She doesn't get it and calls me a weirdo. Skye just laughs. So does Reilly, even though he's so pissed, he's probably not sure what he's laughing at. Swannie and I spend the next while explaining to him how odds work, but he gets confused and giggles into his beer. I wonder if he's taking the piss and actually knows, or if it's because he's embarrassed by his lack of understanding, not helped by his eyes constantly searching for Ellie and Skye, who've gone into the house.

I run my hands over my belly. It feels at maximum capacity, stuffed with burgers, sausages, potato salad, cider, beer, vodka . . . and marshmallows. I wonder how much sugar and calories I've consumed in the last few hours, a thought that's quickly quashed by Reilly thrusting a can of Carlsberg in my hand. I put it down on the table, unopened.

"I'll be back in a minute, man. I need to go to the little boys' room."

I walk up the garden in as straight a line as possible, take time to navigate the patio steps so I don't land on my arse, and then weave my way through unfamiliar faces in the dining room and into the hall. Kev's got his lips pressed into the bathroom door jamb.

"Judy? Are you alright in there? Fuckin' talk to me, will you? Tell me you're alright."

"What's happening, Kev? I'm needing in, man."

"It's Judy. She's been at a baby shower and has come back pissed out her face."

"I wondered where she'd been," I say. "You alright, Judes?"

"That you, Jackie?" she says.

"Yeah, and he's just won £120," Kev says.

"Let him in."

"What?"

"Jack. Let him in."

"How the fuck am *I* supposed to let him in? The lock's on your side, you numpty."

After some fumbling around, the lock clunks open. "Let Jack in."

"Look at the nick of you," Kev says, pointing at her slumped against the wall, her face white, eyes half shut.

"I'll be fine, I'll be fine," she slurs. "I just need somebody to sit with me for a while. You go back to your birthday party."

"I'll make sure she's alright, Kev" I say, stepping over her. I put the toilet seat down and sit on it.

"Shut the door," she says, not even looking at him. "Go back to the party."

Kev mutters something under his breath and shuts the door. Judy forces her body up just enough to lock it and then flops back down like the toys in *Toy Story* when a human walks in the room.

"Ouch, where did that radiator come from?" Judy says, rubbing her head.

"Good baby shower was it then, Judes?"

"Aw, Jackie, it was just the best. I love celebrating new life, so I do."

"That's good, hen." I'm not that sure what else to say.

"You know about me and Kev, don't you, Jack?"

" . . . "

"You know – that it's pretty much over . . . and that nobody really knows. The girls are fine with it, though. I'm really impressed with how chilled out Ellie's been about everything, she's very understanding. And Skye, well, she's just getting on with things, going out and that, living her life, not letting it bother her, you know. You see, Jack, there's only so long you can live a lie and then one day you just tell yourself enough is enough. Don't get me wrong," – she throws a hand into the air – "Kev is a lovely guy, aaaaaa lovely guy, so he is, but he's just not for me long term, you know. We want different things in life, and when you realise that, you've got to stop living a lie, don't you think? Got to stop taking the piss out yourself, man up and deal with things head on."

I just sit and listen, looking at her, the food and booze swirling about in my belly. She's been talking to the side of the bath. She could probably look at me, but it'd sap too much of what little energy she has left.

"The barbecue is, like, my final thing. Fifty's a big deal, you know, and I wanted to do something for him, a last nice deed as his wife, a kinda appreciation for his efforts in trying to make things work. We'll stay pals, Jack. None of us are bitter and we still care about each other, you know. We just can't see the rest of our lives together."

"And is Kev the same?" I ask, fidgeting with the toilet roll holder.

"Yeah. Yeah, he's the same . . . Why, hasn't he said anything to you?"

"Bits here and there, but nothing as solid as not spending the rest of your lives together."

She tries to sit up a bit but ends up back in the same position, which makes me chuckle. "You know what I'm looking forward to, though, Jackie boy? Being single again. Just think of all the men out there I can date. Millions of them. Big hunks and silver foxes, George Clooney types and all that. It'll be brilliant. I'll need to set up one of them fish in the sea account thingies on the computer."

"You mean *Plenty of Fish*," I laugh. "I wouldn't expect to find your George Clooney on there, though, hen. You're more likely to find, well . . . folk like me."

"Are you on there? Noooo way! Is that how you're so, like, popular and confident and that? You know something, Jack – you've got this aura about you. An aura that you get some on a regular basis." She manages to look up. "And I find that incredibly attractive."

I see Ellie in her drunken eyes and the furrow in her forehead is a carbon copy of Skye's.

"I can see that sparkle in your eye! Come on down here and give me a cuddle and tell me everything's going to be alright, like what they do in the movies."

I laugh, embarrassed. I can't do it. It just wouldn't be right.

But she *is* gorgeous.

She opens her arms and looks up again. "Come on."

At first, the knocks on the door are light and intermittent. "Is there anyone in there?" I hear Reilly say. "Does anyone know if there's something wrong with this door?" Then they get louder and more rapid. "Come on, is there anyone in there? I really need a pee!"

Benny Lying Down

My pals were either busy or didn't fancy it, so I just went myself. I felt really self-conscious and kept wondering if people were looking at me thinking *Ha, look at No-Pals over there*. I sent a text to Sam, who I hadn't spoken to in ages. It's not that I particularly wanted to make contact, I just wanted to be seen to be doing something other than just walking around on my own.

> Hi, long time no c, how r u? Still
> working in PR? Am in-between things
> at the mo. How's your dog?

I thought about Benny and wished I was more like him. He walks into pubs and talks to random strangers; goes on holiday himself; buys single concert tickets. I remember I asked him why, and he said 'Well, it's a concert, so it's not like I'll actually be there myself. Plus I'm hardly going to be making polite conversation while Muse are blowing my ears off, am I?'

> Hello stranger, wot a random text,
> I thought u were dead lol ☺ Yup,
> still in PR yawn. Molly died I'm
> afraid, ate slug pellets at my pals

BBQ, innocent mistake but gutted ☹
Great to hear from u tho. Wots the
latest? Sam x

The sun was out so the park was busy. Some guys had their tops off and six-packs on show and I wondered if they'd worked hard at it, or if they were just lucky. I walked past a giant inflatable paddling pool and was reminded of how great it was to be a kid and get such a buzz from simply bouncing up and down in water. I made my way to the hotdog van. I wanted something else to do with my hands.

"What can I get you?" said the smiley man in the white hat and stripy apron.

"A hotdog, please."

"Would you like onions?"

"Yes, please."

The man picked up his oven mitt, lifted a dripping metal lid and picked out a hotdog with his tongs. He placed it in a bun and added a generous helping of onions from the grill.

"There we are," he said, placing it on the counter wrapped in napkins. "That's £2.80 please."

"Thanks." I handed him a fiver, suspicious at the price. I had paid through the nose for a hotdog at these things before.

"£2.20 change. Thanks very much. Enjoy!"

I walked away from the van and, looking over at the performance area, I removed the napkins and took a bite.

"Oh, my God!" I looked closely at what I had bitten into and walked back to the van.

"Hello again," said the man, still smiling. "Everything okay?"

"Eh, yes . . . only, I asked for a hotdog and I don't think that's what you've given me."

"Ha! You're not the first person to say that! Would you like your money back?"

"No, not at all. This is delicious!"

"Why, thank you. It's one of my finest sausages. 85% pork."

"So why would you call this a hotdog?" I asked.

"Because that's what people buy at these things, isn't it?" he said. "And I serve them in hotdog buns with onions and people can put mustard and ketchup on them if they want to, just like a hotdog."

"But this is way better than any hotdog! This is the best sausage I've ever tasted!"

"Well, I'm pleased to hear that. It's great to have another happy customer. Oh, excuse me for now . . . Yes, madam, what can I get you?"

"Two hotdogs please," the woman said.

Lifting the dripping metal lid again, he gave me a nod and a smile which I returned before walking over to the grass where I sat cross-legged and made my hotdog last as long as possible.

The place filled up quickly. I watched the local radio station set up a small stage to the right of the performance area and there were kids in costumes with painted faces rehearsing a dance on the grass. Their red-headed leader was clapping to keep them in time, intermittently shouting words of encouragement.

I rested my elbows on the grass and stretched out my legs. It was funny how I felt less self-conscious on the ground. I lay there people-watching with the sun on my face and wondered if this was how Benny felt all the time. I decided that next time I end up going to an event on my own, or I'm first to arrive at the pub, I'll just pretend I'm Benny lying down.

A group of girls walked towards me, each of them wearing vibrant summer dresses. One had a cowboy hat and long dark hair nearly down to her waist. Another had long blonde hair, red lipstick to match her frock and sunglasses that took up half her face. I thought the third girl was an Inuit. She had long pigtails which rested like ropes on her purple polka-dot dress, attire alien to her native climate. They looked so cool, like they were in a band about to be photographed for a magazine.

"Do you mind if we sit here?" asked the one in the cowboy hat.

"No, of course not," I said, surprised at being asked. After all, it wasn't like I owned the grass. They sat down and the blonde took a flask out of her bag.

"Are you from around here?"

"Yeah, I only live five minutes from here, actually." I was a little apprehensive at them being at my level, that they'd work out I was here alone.

"Oh, cool!" she said. I couldn't work out if she was being genuine or patronising. "It must be great living so close to such a lovely spot."

"Eh, yeah, I suppose. So I take it you're not from around here then?"

She laughed. "No, I'm American. From LA. Just here on vacation."

I felt my face flush. I knew she was American from her accent, but she hadn't picked up on the sarcasm in my question.

"Cool," I said. "If you don't mind me asking, what made you come here?"

"We have a friend who moved here to get married and so we thought, well why not take a proper vacation while we're at it, huh?"

"The wedding was last weekend," said the Inuit-looking girl, leaning over, "in this humongous castle up north. And oh my God, do you guys know how to party!"

"Yeah, we do have that reputation," I laughed, surprised at how American she sounded. "I take it you all had a good time then?"

"Hell, yeah!" the girl in the cowboy hat said. "My hangover's only just gone now!"

"Speaking of which, Mary-Lee." The blonde passed her a plastic cup.

"Ah, good call, sister!"

"Would you like to join us in the consumption of some fine bourbon?" the blonde asked me, putting on a mock formal voice.

"Sure, why not," I laughed, and she poured a generous amount into a plastic cup and passed it over.

"Here's to beautiful sunny days!" We clinked cups, even though plastic doesn't clink, and downed them together. I felt the fire in my throat and instant buzz.

"God damn!" said Mary-Lee.

"Ladies and gentleman," came the amplified deep voice of a man in a checked shirt standing at a microphone. We looked over to the stage as the blonde girl poured more bourbon into our cups. "Please put your hands together for Patsy McLean and The Little Rascals!"

People clapped as a skinny girl with long dark hair, who looked a bit like Mary-Lee – only younger and without the cowboy hat – stepped onto the stage, next to a large kettle drum. The kids assembled with their backs to the audience and their red-haired leader crouched down at the front of the stage. The park fell quiet. The long-haired girl, who I assumed was Patsy McLean, picked up two beaters which looked like cavemen's clubs and beat the drum with such gusto that the audience jumped with fright. People looked at each other to laugh off the shock as the kids burst into their choreography. The blonde handed me another cup of bourbon. And we watched the kids.

"They are amazing," Mary-Lee said.

And they were. Their timing was perfect, each of them in sync with the beat and each other. Their red-haired leader was nodding and holding up double thumbs, clearly delighted at how well they were doing. Patsy's beat grew louder and more intense, to the extent that her slight pink face disappeared under her hair as the dynamics of the performance swelled to a beautiful, spine-tingling conclusion.

Patsy pounded the drum for the last time and there was a second or two of silence as people absorbed what they had just seen. Everyone rose to their feet and cheered, like we were in a cheesy film where the central character was useless throughout, but somehow managed to shine on the big day.

"Woooooooooo!" Mary-Lee hollered, clapping above her head.

"Awesome! Frickin' awesome!" the blonde girl shouted, throwing her fist round in a circle.

I felt a fuzzy warmth. These American girls were lapping up stuff that was on my doorstep, stuff people from my town either took for granted or paid no attention to. And although I felt a little guilty for thinking it, part of me was pleased none of my friends had come with me.

"Your country is wicked," the Inuit said, passing me another bourbon.

"Thanks. I'm glad you're enjoying it."

"We've still got six days before we fly home. Where else do you recommend we go?"

"Well . . ." But before I could say any more, we were cut off by the revving engines of motorbikes. The crowd cheered and whooped. Once the engines had settled to a purr, the man with the deep voice and the checked shirt tapped the microphone.

"Ladies and gentleman, please give a warm welcome to Davey's Daredevil Dirtbikes!"

Everyone clapped. The girls had joy on their faces. The sun was still shining and I was loving the buzz from the bourbon.

The show was amazing. I'd seen similar stunts on TV, but hearing the roar of the engines, smelling the fumes and being part of the crowd made it a completely different experience. In-between stunts, I sent Benny a quick text.

> How's the holiday goin?   Hope you've met some nice folk

Just as I was about to slip my phone back into my pocket, it vibrated. Sam.

> Was wonderin why u contacted me after all this time. Was that jst an innocent txt or are u lookin for something more? I always liked u back at uni. Would be up for meetin 4 a drink if u fancy x x

"Shit."
"Everything okay?" Mary-Lee asked.

"Yeah, everything's cool."

"These guys are blowing my frickin' mind!"

I looked around and everybody was enjoying themselves. At these things there's usually someone letting the side down, but I couldn't see trouble anywhere. There was a big queue at the hotdog van and my new American friends, who were feeding me bourbon like I was one of their besties, were shouting 'Awesome!' at the bikers, even though they couldn't be heard. But it didn't matter. They were just so happy to be part of something spectacular. And free. I felt emotional, brought on, no doubt, by the bourbon. But it was just brilliant. I was Benny lying down, and I never wanted it to end.